# Never Say Forever

## By
## Robert Fisher

Never Say Forever Robert Fisher
Copyright© 2022 La Maison Publishing
ISBN: 978-1-970153-38-5
Distribution: Ingram Book Company

Cover Art by Aaron Williams

Maison

La Maison Publishing
Vero Beach, Florida
The Hibiscus City
lamaisonpublishing@gmail.com

# Chapter 1
## Armageddon in a Briefcase

General Dolan waited anxiously on the bench, in the moonlit park in Prague. His left hand was clenched tightly on the handle of the small gray briefcase. He looked around for his contact, a man he knew only as Counselor Blakelock, but saw nothing in the omnipresent darkness that enveloped the park. He checked his watch, it read 10:30 pm.

"He's late," grunted Dolan as he reached into his jacket and pulled out a cigarette and lighter.

As he put the cigarette in his mouth and prepared to light it he heard a voice from behind him say "You know those things will kill you right?"

The cigarette fell out of his mouth as Dolan turned around to face him, a surprised look on his face. "Finally, you're here," said Dolan quickly regaining his composure.

Counselor Blakelock was a tall younger man with sharp features. He was dressed in a black trench coat, dress shirt with a tie, gloves, pants and a silver belt around his waist. On his head was a wide brimmed black fedora with a gray band. Dolan noticed the silver briefcase in his left hand. "That I am General, do you have it?" asked the Counselor.

"Yes, I assume the money is in the briefcase," replied General Dolan.

"One hundred million as we agreed" said Counselor Blakelock as he held up the briefcase.

"Good then let's get this over with, I want to be rid of this damn thing," replied Dolan.

Cautiously, Blakelock took the briefcase from Dolan. He opened it and smiled, pleased at the contents.

"I hope you realize how dangerous that is," said Dolan.

"Your loss is our gain" said Blakelock smugly.

Dolan grimaced at the remark, "what about the money?"

"Ah yes the money, that which makes the world go round," said Counselor Blakelock as he closed the briefcase.

"I didn't come here for philosophy," complained General Dolan.

"Does anyone?" replied Blakelock as he handed his briefcase to Dolan.

Dolan accepted the briefcase and opened it. Inside were rows of hundred dollar bills. Dolan smiled, satisfied as he closed the briefcase. "Enjoy your retirement General," said Counselor Blakelock.

"I intend to," said Dolan as he walked away from him.

"I'm sure you do," muttered Counselor Blakelock. He reached into the interior pocket of his black trench coat and pulled out a silenced Glock 19 pistol.

He aimed it at the back of Dolans head and pulled the trigger twice. Instantly Dolan fell on the floor face first. Casually, Counselor Blakelock walked over to him and picked up his briefcase.

"Nothing personal, we can't have any loose ends," he said.

He reached into his pants pocket, pulled out a cellphone and dialed a number. After a few rings the voice of his employer answered. "Mr. Two, this is Counselor Blakelock. Please notify Mr. Zero that I have the package, Project: GHOST FIRE is proceeding as planned."

"Understood, return to headquarters immediately" said the voice of Mr. Two before hanging up. Blakelock returned the phone to his pocket and left the park.

***

Like most agents of MI6's elite black ops division, Equinox, Nigel Solo tried to keep his emotions out of his missions. When an assignment became personal, an agents judgment was clouded usually ending in disaster for the agent. He had been trying to keep his emotions out of his current assignment, considering that he had a history with this target in particular. He sat back in his chair in the small office at the British embassy in Dubai. He looked outside the window before returning his gaze to the folder on his desk that he had procured from the local police department.

The file concerned a shootout in a local bazaar two weeks ago involving his target. The mission was best summed up by its initials L.A.T, which stood for Locate And Terminate an enemy of the crown by any means. He had carried out L.A.T. orders before, but this one was different. Not only because of his history with the target, but because it had come directly from the Prime Minister. He was frustrated that he had managed to be one step behind her.

Three months ago, he received word that she had been sighted at an airport in Australia. So he went there to find a lead, but instead found nothing. Two months later he received word that she was in New York traveling with a Chinese man, who was affiliated with the Heise She Li Triad, but he had just missed her. It was the same several days later in Tokyo, where she was sighted on a security camera in the harbor.

Two weeks ago she had been sighted in Dubai, but once again by the time he arrived she was gone. While in Dubai, Nigel had been residing in the British Embassy waiting for any word of any new sightings of her from the Director of Equinox. According to the file he had read regarding the shootout, she was sighted in a car that an unidentified man and woman ran into before driving off. He picked up the small cup of tea next to the folder and drank it. He returned the cup to the desk and picked up the folder, deciding to skim through it once again in case he missed anything.

Most of it focused on the details of the shootout, but clipped to the third page via paperclip was a grainy black and white picture of her in the front passenger seat of the car taken by a street camera. As grainy as the picture was it was definitely her, once again inexplicably dressed in the same nun outfit she had been photographed wearing in Australia and New York. In the picture she was as beautiful and probably still as dangerous as ever. She had been called a terrorist by MI6 and nicknamed the Devil Woman by the IRA. Although Nigel knew her by her real name: Siobhan Costello.

# Chapter 2
## Stray Bullets

The Devils Sea exists within the waters of the Philippine Sea. Within the Devils Sea lies Sankan Island, a refuge for both the criminal and the desperate. Control of the city, on the islands southern half, is divided between the Heise She Li Triad from China and the Russian Vasilev Syndicate. Simon Kane reclined in his chair in the office that Deng, the head of the Triads Sankan branch, had provided him. The office was located on the upper floors of the Triads building. It was a small but fully furnished office with everything Simon needed.

Ever since he had returned to Sankan two weeks ago he had been training and assessing the skills of his team. The team was assembled by Deng and led by Simon with the goal of bringing down the enigmatic criminal organization known as the Networc. On his desk were three folders containing all the information the Triad had assembled on Simon's new teammates. There was Mack Roycewicz, a former Army Ranger turned international assassin who would serve as the team's muscle and connection to the Guild.

Then there was Mack's friend Dennis Faraday, who according to his file was an expert in computers, making him the team's technical support and hacker. Finally, there was Siobhan Costello, a former IRA terrorist and assassin who faked her death and became a catholic nun. Due to the reputation she had in the IRA Simon considered her the team's hand-to-hand combat expert. Despite their differences, Simon had managed to get them to work together as an effective unit. However, what troubled him was the fact that the team was missing something it needed to be truly effective: a sniper.

Technically he and Mack were good enough, but good enough was not sufficient for what they needed to accomplish.

Simon knew all too well how dangerous the Networcs operatives were and what they were capable of. Months ago, while on a mission in Belarus an agent of the Networc killed his wife, Sheila. Simon swore to avenge her death and was thus recruited by the closest thing the Networc had to a rival: The Triad. In response the Triad had dispatched agents all over the world to find any trace of the Networc and they had found nothing. All they knew was that the organization was led by a man called Mr. Zero.

However, the more immediate problem was the sniper. Simon had a meeting with Deng later in the day regarding the matter. He looked out the window. The city was less a city and more a series of dilapidated slums populated with those desperate or insane enough to live there. The islands skyline was dominated by two skyscraper's, one was the Triads building and the other belonged to the Syndicate. Beyond the city was a small mountain range and forest.

Simon checked his watch and saw that it was time for the meeting. He shrugged, picked up the folders and walked out of the office and took the elevator to Deng's office on the top floor.

Deng's office was an impressive larger room with bookshelves on the left and right walls. Deng's wooden desk was in front of a massive panoramic window. In front of the desk were two wooden chairs meant for guests. Seated behind the desk was Deng. He was dressed in his usual attire a white dress shirt, black tie trench coat and pants. Simon was wearing his black dress shirt, dark green pants and dark blue trench coat. Deng looked up at Simon as he walked into the room.

"Have a seat," said Deng as he leaned back in his chair. Simon sat down.

"Let's cut to the chase, this team you've assembled is good but we need a sniper," said Simon bluntly.

Deng raised his eyebrow surprised at Simon's words. "What about Siobhan and Mack, or yourself?"

"Siobhan and Mack are good but good isn't enough, we need someone excellent," answered Simon. "And as for me, well my sniping skills aren't what they used to be" continued Simon as he gestured to the black eye patch covering the remains of his right eye. "Fortunately, I know a guy."

"Who?" asked Deng.

"Deon Bowman, he's an old friend of mine that I used to work with at Langley" answered Simon.

"Can he be trusted?" asked Deng.

Simon felt annoyed by the question but nonetheless understood Deng's reason for asking it. "I'd trust him with my life".

Deng sighed as he leaned back in his chair. "Let me rephrase that, would you trust him with the lives of the rest of the team?" replied Deng.

"Absolutely," replied Simon.

"Where is he?" Deng asked.

"Knowing him, back home in San Francisco," answered Simon.

Deng was about to speak but Simon knew exactly what he was going to say. "Before you say anything, I'll contact him myself" answered Simon.

"And if he says no?" asked Deng.

Simon could hear the subtle skepticism in Deng's question. "Then he says no and we use Mack or Siobhan as a sniper, maybe find someone from the Guild," answered Simon.

"Do what you have to," grunted Deng. "Though you should hurry, after all we could get actionable intel on the Networc any minute."

"Thanks for the advice," said Simon dismissively.

He stood up and turned to leave when another question occurred to him. He almost didn't ask it but it had been burning in him ever since she left. "Deng, how's Mai?"

Deng shrugged, "You know, I can't answer that".

"Yeah, that's what I thought," answered Simon as he walked out of Deng's office.

On the way back to his office, his thoughts quickly shifted from Mai to the more relevant question of how he was going to contact Deon. For former Silhouette agents like Simon it is illegal to leave the United States. Any agent that did would be deemed an enemy of the state, hunted down and killed by agents of Silhouettes elite internal affairs agency, Blacklist Protocol. In the six months that he'd been working with the Triad he had often wondered why Blacklist protocol hadn't tried to kill him yet. As for Deon, he decided to send him an E-mail asking him if he wanted in.

Still the questions nagged at him. There was no doubt in his mind that Silhouette, and by extension Blacklist Protocol, knew where he was. So why had he been allowed to live for so long? What kind of game were the CIA and Silhouette playing and how much longer would it be before they decided to remove him from the board altogether?

# Chapter 3
## Missing Arrow

Unbeknownst to all but the President, Director of the CIA and the Secretary of Defense is a covert fifth branch of the Central Intelligence Agency. Known as Silhouette, this branch is responsible for carrying out black operations deemed necessary for the national security of the United States. It is essentially a private army with operatives taken from each branch of the military, Special Forces and intelligence community answerable directly and exclusively to the President.

Silhouette is divided into four branches, each branch referred to as tables. Table One is its command branch that answers to the President and assigns missions among other duties. Table Two is Silhouettes research and development branch known to the world as Twilight Industries the proceeds of which are used to fund Silhouette. Table Three, also known as Blacklist Protocol, is Silhouettes internal affairs branch, which also served as bodyguards for General Connors. Table Four is the division responsible for field agents and operations such as Task Force 666

Silhouettes Director, General Mark Connors, waited patiently in the conference room in Silhouette headquarters, below the CIA's building in Langley, Virginia. In the middle of the room was a long wooden conference table, on the left wall was a large computer screen. Seated across from the table from Connors was the Director of the CIA, a surly bureaucrat named David Campbell. They had been waiting for the President (colloquially referred to as POTUS) and the Secretary of Defense (colloquially referred to as SECDEF). Meetings such as this, with the only men in the entire American government aware of Silhouettes existence were rare, but when they did happen it was usually because of a serious crisis requiring Presidential approval of the mission.

Within minutes, the President and Secretary arrived. The President sat at the head of the table while the Secretary sat next to Connors.

The President sighed, "all right gentlemen what is so bad that we had to be called in?" he said in an annoyed tone.

General Connors stood up and walked to the edge of the table towards the computer screen on the wall. "Gentlemen, 48 hours ago a NATO general was found dead in Prague. Investigators determined that he had stolen a file from a NATO base regarding the location of the fourth nuke".

"The what?" asked the President curiously.

"Bullshit, the fourth nuke has never been found," snorted SECDEF.

"Would someone please tell me what the hell the Fourth Nuke is?" asked the President impatiently.

"The short version, Mr. President, is that in 1968 a NATO B-52 bomber, while on patrol, crashed off the coast of Greenland carrying four nuclear weapons," explained the Secretary.

"Naturally, a team was deployed to recover the nukes however we only found three of the four bombs," continued the Secretary. "We believed the missing bomb was lost forever in the North Sea"

"Not forever," muttered General Connors.

The President took a deep breath and pinched the skin above his nose out of annoyance. "Would you care to explain that comment General?"

"Yes Sir, at the time the missing bomb was impossible to find, however a few years ago we managed to locate it using a satellite codenamed: Black Knight," answered the General.

"Ever since we found it I've been keeping an eye on it" said Connors as he pulled a small remote out of his pocket. He aimed it at the screen and pressed a button. Instantly a picture of a black oval surrounded by orange rings appeared on the screen.

"What am I looking at?" asked the President.

"Mr. President, this is a radiation analysis we obtained via satellite. The black oval shaped object in the middle of the picture is the Fourth Nuke," answered Connors.

"It doesn't matter it's impossible for anyone to get it," said the Secretary.

"Wrong again, you see, we believe the Networc is trying to recover it" said General Connors.

There was an annoyed groan coming from Campbell at the mention of the word Networc. "Mr. President, with all due respect ever since Operation Fire Breaker this man has directed all of Silhouettes resources towards finding this ghost he calls the Networc. He's even allowed a rogue agent to run rampant because he thinks that he'll find them" said Campbell.

"Mr. President, contrary to Director Campbell's opinions we have uncovered evidence that this organization does exist and has the means to recover this weapon" protested General Connors.

"I see, and you're sure they are after the weapon?" asked the President.

Connors sighed. "At present no, however we noticed that a deep sea diving ship belonging to Prometheus Technologies is hanging around the site."

"Which proves that someone is interested in recovering the bomb," answered Connors. "And, what I am sure of Mr. President is that we cannot allow the Networc or anyone else to get that weapon".

The President was silent for a full minute. "Alright General, I'm convinced, get those plans back".

"However, I don't want Silhouette involved directly understand?" said the President.

"Yes Sir," said Connors, a plan was starting to form in Connors head. "However we will need to recover the bomb to prevent this from happening again".

"Fine. Once you have the plans use Twilight Industries to recover it" replied the President.

"Good, now this meeting is over" said the President as he and the Secretary of Defense stood up and left.

Campbell shrugged and walked out of the room with Connors following behind him. Connors rode the elevator back to his office, his mind focused on the plan. The elevator opened into Connors office. As soon as

Connors stepped out of the elevator his bookcase automatically slid in front of it with a barely audible mechanical hum concealing the entrance to Silhouettes underground headquarters. The General walked to his desk, sat down and thought. The President had forbidden him from using Silhouette agents to recover the file which left him with no other option. He got on his computer and accessed a file marked PARTY LIST, containing intel on every member of the International Assassins Guild.

Silhouette had a long, complicated history with the Guild as did similar agencies across the world. The Guild functioned as a trade union for the world's most elite hitmen, freelance assassins and mercenaries. He scrolled through the names until he found the one he was looking for: KATYUSHA. According to her file she was currently in Spain. He pulled out his phone and pressed a small button that automatically encrypted the call.

Then he dialed the number that the Guild had assigned KATYUSHA. After a few seconds of ringing he was greeted with a seductive female Russian accent that made him wish he was younger.

"My name is NARRATOR; I have a job for you. The offer has a 24 hour time limit and money is no object" said Connors.

"I'm listening," said the voice.

Connors smiled, "I need you to steal a drive from the headquarters of Prometheus Technologies,"

The phone was silent for a half minute, "I know who you are NARRATOR, and I know who you work for, you have access to information I want," said the voice.

Connors had expected this since KATYUSHA was a former member of the Russian equivalent of Silhouette known as Red Curtain. She also had numerous encounters with Simon Kane when he was a member of Silhouette. "It depends on the information you're looking for"

"You have intel on a terrorist organization called Aquarius, I want it as well as one million dollars," said KATYUSHA.

"Aquarius intel only" Connors replied sternly; the phone went quiet for several minutes.

"500,000 and the intel" said KATYUSHA.

There was no way of knowing but Connors was positive she was smiling on the other side of the phone. "Then I guess we have a deal."

"Excellent, send me the details of the job" replied KATYUSHA before abruptly hanging up.

Connors then began to type an E-mail containing a censored version of the plan he had formed, omitting things such as the CIA, Silhouette and nuclear weapons. He clicked on Send and the message went off into the digital sea like a message in a bottle.

# Chapter 4
## The Molotov Gambit

Sasha Molotova placed her phone on the small table next to her reclining chair. She closed her eyes and leaned into the chair. She had just returned from a job in Yemen and had chosen to spend a few weeks relaxing at her Spanish villa. At moments like this, she thought about the path her life had taken, from starving orphan on the streets of Moscow to Spetsnaz commando to Red Curtain agent and finally to member of the International Assassins Guild.

She was a beautiful tall Russian woman with the voluptuous figure of a supermodel and the athletic muscles of an Olympic gymnast. Covering her right eye was a black eye patch. She had lost her eye years ago on a mission for Red Curtain. Having just accepted the job offer from Connors, she had returned to lying in her chair on the patio in her red bathing suit enjoying the sun. Just as she was beginning to fall asleep, her phone suddenly began ringing incessantly, rousing her from a sound sleep. She grunted, annoyed at the interruption and picked up the phone.

It was an E-mail from Connors containing the details of the job he had hired her for, as well as a PDF file containing the plans for the facility. According to the E-mail the job was fairly simple, she was to break into a secure vault at the headquarters of a Finnish company known as Prometheus Technologies. Then steal a computer drive and deliver it to General Connors where she would receive her payment. She was curious as to why Connors wouldn't just dispatch a Silhouette agent to do it but she brushed her curiosity aside. The reasons for the job didn't matter to her. All that mattered to her was the what, the where and occasionally who. She read it carefully twice and then with a shrug stood up and walked into her bedroom.

She walked straight to her chifferobe and pulled out her suitcase. She also removed some traveling clothes namely a pair of black slacks and a black shirt. She spent the next several minutes getting dressed and packing. She opened her suitcase and pressed a small button that revealed a secret compartment with a box inside. She removed the box, sat on the bed and placed the box on her lap.

She opened it and removed her weapon of choice: a scoped Mauser C96 broom handle pistol. She began examining it, when she was satisfied with the guns condition, she returned it to the black box. She put the box back in the secret compartment, then she checked her combat suit and other weapons. Her field attire consisted of red combat boots, a red belt, black leather gloves and a black spandex body suit.

Pleased at finding that her suit and clothing were intact, she checked her knife and backup weapons; she was pleased to see they were in fine working order. Usually Sasha's contracts were assassinations of various kinds of people for those who could afford to pay. However, thanks to the training and experience she gained from several years as a field agent for Red Curtain, she was capable of performing a robbery like this. She checked her phone for the first available flight to Helsinki and saw that there was a flight leaving in four hours out of Adolfo Suarez Madrid-Barajas airport in Madrid.

She sighed; annoyed that she couldn't find a better flight but she booked a seat on the plane nonetheless. She checked one final time to make sure she had everything she needed. She closed her suitcase and walked out of the villa to her car.

***

The roof of the Triads building contained a small garden with a stone walkway that led to a cul-de-sac. In the middle of the cul-de-sac was a table and three chairs. Deng sat at the table looking out at the city of Sankan. Beyond the city, he could see the long dormant volcano, Mount Soka. It loomed over Sankan Island like a God, angry at the den of villainy and sin that is Sankan. Behind him he heard two sets of footsteps approaching, he turned around and saw his assistant, Mazin, and behind him the imposing figure of Siobhan Costello. She was dressed in her black and white nun's habit with her gold cross necklace around her neck, while Mazin was wearing a black and white suit and carrying a manila folder with him.

"Have a seat, Sister Costello," said Deng affably.

"Why have you summoned me here Deng?" asked Siobhan, in her lyrical Irish accent, as she and Mazin sat down at the table.

"We have a problem," said Deng. "Mazin, the file please."

Mazin handed him the file and he opened it and started reading. "It appears that your old life is catching up to your new one," said Deng looking up at her.

"How so?" asked Siobhan.

"We've discovered that MI6 has dispatched an agent to kill you," said Deng.

Siobhan sighed. In the back of her mind she knew the British would find out she had faked her death and send someone to kill her as punishment for the terrorist attacks she had committed during her time with the I.R.A. "Usually when people find out that there is a target on their head they act a little more emotional," said Deng.

"It's all part of God's plan for me," said Siobhan lightly. "How long have you known?"

"I've had my suspicions that we were being watched ever since our trip to New York two months ago," answered Deng. "At first I thought it was the Networc so I asked Mazin to look into it".

Deng handed her the folder, Siobhan opened it and saw a black and white picture of a tall man in a gray suit taken from across the street.

"The man in the picture is Nigel Solo, codename: SABRE. I suggest you keep it with you in case you see him," advised Deng.

"I don't need the picture," said Siobhan as she returned the folder to Deng.

"This is my problem. I'll handle it," said Siobhan.

"It was your problem, I'm concerned that this man might become our problem," said Deng.

"I wouldn't worry about it, if he does find me and interferes with my mission, I will eliminate him," said Siobhan.

"And that mission is…" asked Deng.

"To serve the Lord," said Siobhan calmly.

Deng grinned, "Sankan is a hell of a place to start".

She smiled faintly at Deng's comment. "So were Sodom and Gomorrah," replied Siobhan with a grin.

"Touché," said Deng.

"Is that all?" asked Siobhan.

"Yes. That'll be all, let's keep this development between us for now" said Deng.

Siobhan nodded as she stood up and walked away. Once she was gone Mazin looked at Deng. "Hard to believe that she used to be called the Devil Woman" said Mazin.

"After living here, not very" said Deng. "Sankan has a way of making people numb to the evils and madness of the world".

Mazin nodded, knowing what he meant. "By the way Sir, do you really think one MI6 agent like this Nigel person could present a threat to our plans?"

"He's not MI6," said Deng.

"What do you mean?" asked Mazin.

"I'm willing to bet that he's really an Equinox agent," said Deng.

"Equinox? That makes sense if the Brits wanted someone like her dead then they wouldn't use MI6 directly considering the potential blowback," Mazin replied.

"Exactly, they'd use Equinox," said Deng.

"Especially for someone like her," said Mazin.

"Point is, Equinox or not I don't want anyone involving themselves in this," said Deng.

"So what do you want to do then?" asked Mazin.

Deng thought for a minute, "the only thing we can do is keep an eye on Siobhan because if this is Equinox, then they'll go to any length to kill her," said Deng.

"Yes Sir" said Mazin.

"By the way any word from Kane?" asked Deng.

"Not yet Sir" answered Mazin.

"Damn," muttered Deng as the two men stood up and walked back inside the building.

# Chapter 5
## Small World After All

Simon Kane was glad to be off of Sankan. He had managed to convince Deng to fly him out to Taipei where he would rendezvous with Deon. They had arranged to meet at a small restaurant called Coffee Megane in the Da'an District in the city. It was an out of the way café hidden amongst the concrete metropolis of Taipei. The interior was composed of wooden tables and chairs and a bar. The restaurant had only been open for an hour so it was relatively empty.

Simon had been waiting at a table facing the entrance drinking tea and reading a magazine. Occasionally, he would glance up to see if Deon walked in. Simon was wearing dark green pants, a black buttoned shirt and his dark blue trench coat. He looked up just as Deon entered. He was a large, muscular African American man with short black hair.

He was dressed in a yellow t-shirt and black pants. Simon raised his hand so that he would see him. Deon smiled and walked over to him. Simon tossed the magazine down on the table as Deon sat down across the table from him.

"When are you gonna get rid of that ugly ass coat?" asked Deon jokingly with a cocky smile.

"When you get rid of that ugly ass shirt" replied Simon sarcastically.

The two men looked at each other sternly for half a minute before laughing quietly.

"It's been too long MONOLITH," said Deon.

Simon smiled at hearing his old codename from his days with Silhouette.

"What have you been up to?" Deon inquired.

"It's a long story, ROUNDABOUT," said Simon.

Deon grinned at hearing his old codename as well. "Is this all about getting payback for what those Networc guys did to Sheila?"

Simon nodded.

"Well, I'm in," replied Deon.

"Obviously, if I may ask why now, why not eight months ago?" asked Simon.

Deon was silent for almost a full minute. "We've never been strangers to death Simon, but after Sheila died I couldn't take it anymore so I tried to forget about it," continued Deon. "But I couldn't, so when I got your E-mail I jumped at the chance to get some payback for her".

"Glad to hear it, you do know that Blacklist Protocol will come after you now right?" asked Simon.

"Let them. To be honest I thought they'd have killed you by now," said Deon.

"Funny thing is they haven't," said Simon.

"Weird," Deon muttered.

"I don't know what's going on at Langley but the odds are someone wants us alive," said Simon.

"Must be Connors," Deon grunted.

"Bigger question is why," asked Simon.

"An even bigger question is how are the two of us going to bring down an organization that not even Connors and Silhouette could find?" asked Deon.

Simon smiled, "what makes you think it's just the two of us?"

"What do you mean?" asked Deon.

"The short version is that the Heise She Li Triad and the Networc are old enemies so after I did a…favor for them on Sankan Island they agreed to gather a team to help me take on the Networc," answered Simon.

"And me?" asked Deon.

"Deon, you're one of the best snipers the Marines ever had, we need you," Simon explained.

"Well as true as that is, and it is, I've got to ask who is on this team the Triad assembled?" asked Deon.

"Let's just say they're specialists," Simon answered.

"Any of them knuckledraggers?" asked Deon, using the nickname Silhouettes agents used to refer to each other.

"None of them are ex-agency but they are good, really good," Simon explained.

"Ok. So where are we going to meet these "specialists"?" asked Deon.

"Sankan Island," answered Simon.

"Sankan? That shit hole?" Deon replied incredulously.

"Yeah, the Triads building on Sankan is essentially our home base until they find actionable intel on the Networc," said Simon reassuringly.

"That's some home base. Was hell unavailable?" asked Deon sardonically.

Simon laughed at Deon's remark. "Be that as it may, are you still in?"

"To the bitter end," replied Deon.

"Let's hope it doesn't come to that," said Simon.

"When do we leave?" asked Deon.

"Immediately, the driver outside is waiting to take us to the airport where a private plane is waiting to fly us back to Sankan," answered Simon.

"I see, I didn't know they had flights to hell," Deon said.

"Neither did I," said Simon dryly.

"I must say Simon, I am excited to see this team of yours," Deon said.

"Ours" corrected Simon.

"Right" grunted Deon. "Well then let's go."

"After you" said Simon as the two men stood up.

Simon quickly paid for his tea, and then walked outside with Deon following behind him. They walked across the street to a black car. As they approached the car, the driver got out and opened the rear passenger door for them. The two men got in, while the driver closed the door and then returned to the driver's seat where he started the engine.

"Swanky car," remarked Deon casually as he studied the interior of the car.

"Wait till you see Deng's office," said Simon.

# Chapter 6
## The Secrets Of The Gods

The headquarters of Prometheus Technologies was just one of many skyscrapers in Helsinki. While the denizens of the city ignored the building as they went about their daily lives, Sasha Molotova had studied it and memorized the blueprints of the structure. Sasha had spent the day devising her plan to surreptitiously enter and exit the plan and now she was ready to implement it. According to the blueprints the vault containing the drive was on the eighteenth floor. She had chosen to enter the building at night when there was barely anyone inside except for guards and cleaning staff.

She had parked her car in the public parking garage across the street from the back of the building. Sasha was dressed in her black cat suit, gloves and dark red boots, hanging from her belt was her holster containing her pistol. Slung across her back was a small backpack containing various tools and clipped to the back of her belt was a small grapple gun. She removed the pistol from her holster and placed it on the dashboard of her rented car. Sasha then reached into one of her belt pockets and pulled out the suppressor for the gun. She casually picked up her gun from the dashboard and screwed the suppressor on tightly. Finally, she returned the gun to her holster, she did not expect to use it, but was prepared to if necessary.

Sasha took a deep breath and stepped out of the car, she was greeted by the cool air of the Scandinavian night. She carefully walked out of the parking garage until she was across the street from the building. Behind the building was a ramp that led to a small parking lot below. At the bottom was a fence hanging from the ceiling that barred entry during non-business hours.

Sasha quickly ran across the street and down the ramp. She reached into one of the pouches on her belt and pulled out a small aerosol can that contained a special kind of acid. She knelt down and lightly shook the can.

Carefully she sprayed the acid on the fence, making an oval shape with the spray. Within seconds the section of the fence she sprayed began to dissolve. Finally, when the acid had finished its work she kicked the fence with her foot and the oval shaped segment of the fence she made fell backward. She smiled, satisfied as she returned the can to her belt. Carefully Sasha crawled through the hole and into the parking garage, once inside she looked around, it was empty and dimly lit. On the far side of the parking lot she could see an elevator.

She walked over to the elevator, pressed the button and when the doors opened she walked inside and selected the floor marked 18. When the doors opened she was facing a dark hallway, gingerly she stepped out of the elevator. The hallway was a series of doors and offices, the omnipresent, almost unsettling, quiet made her feel like she was walking through an ancient tomb. Sasha's training and instincts had been honed to notice sound, even in intense quiet such as this. She stealthily walked down the corridor. In her hyper awareness she suddenly heard the faint tap of approaching footsteps behind her.

Instinctively, she reached for her pistol, but stopped short of drawing it, reasoning it was probably a janitor. She looked around for somewhere to hide as the footsteps got closer. Finally, she saw it on the left wall towards the ceiling: a ventilation grate. There was a small table with a flower pot directly below it. Sasha stood on it and pulled a small screwdriver out of her belt and unscrewed the two screws holding the grate in as quietly as possible.

Quickly but quietly, Sasha crawled into the ventilation shaft. She replaced the grate once she was inside. She waited nervously for the guard to pass, watching him walk past through the grate. Once he was gone, she decided to crawl the rest of the way through the ventilation shaft. She would come out at the next grate where she would be face-to-face with the vault at least according to the blueprints Connors had provided. Using her gymnast skills, she managed to painfully, but successfully, turn around so she would be able to see in front of her.

She looked down the dark ventilation duct and let out a barely audible sigh, annoyed that she would have to crawl through a cramped ventilation shaft as opposed to walking. Slowly she crawled through the ventilation shaft trying not to make a sound. It was not the first time she had been forced to crawl through a cramped space in the name of secrecy but she soldiered on. Finally, she came upon another grate, she looked through the slits and saw the vault door across the room. She smiled having found her quarry.

She reached into her belt and pulled out the same bottle of acid. She backed away from the grate and sprayed it on the four corners of the square grate, being careful to cover her eye. Within seconds the grate fell to the floor with a somewhat loud thud. Sasha easily crawled out of the shaft, glad to finally be out of it. The room was large with a wooden door to the side and brown carpet on the floor.

On the far side of the room was a massive vault door made out of what appeared to be solid steel. On the wall next to the door was a small console that allowed entrance to the vault. Opposite the vault was a wall sized tinted black window. Eagerly she walked over to the vault, intent on cracking the code on the small console next to the door. Suddenly Sasha heard a door creak open and the footsteps of someone walk in.

"That's very impressive, Miss Molotova" said a smug male voice behind her.

Instinctively, Sasha drew her pistol as she turned around, aiming the gun at the man.

"Or would you prefer KATYUSHA?" asked the man.

Sasha glared at him, choosing instead to study his appearance. He was dressed in a black trench coat, dress shirt and pants with a silver gray belt. On his head was a wide-brimmed black fedora with gray band. His hands were behind him, he looked at Sasha with an arrogant smile on his face. Sasha could tell something was different about this man. "How do you know my name?" she asked.

"We know everything about you," said the man.

"You're not with Prometheus, who are you?" asked Sasha strongly.

"You can call me Counselor Blakelock, at least for the few remaining minutes you have left that is," replied the man smugly.

"Is that so?" asked Sasha sarcastically as she tried to come up with a way out.

Counselor Blakelock snapped his fingers and five large men in black combat gear holding assault rifles, they're faces covered by black balaclavas ran into the room. They stood behind Counselor Blakelock and aimed their rifles at her. Little red dots of light appeared on her body coming from the rifles laser sights.

"Yes. Yes it is Miss Molotova," said Blakelock confidently with a hint of smugness.

Sasha considered her options, one look at the body armor on the soldiers told her that her pistol would not be enough to fight them off. She briefly considered shooting Blakelock in the head, but decided against it since those soldiers most likely had orders to shoot her if anything happened to Blakelock.

"If I were you I'd drop your gun," he said.

Suddenly, Sasha had an idea, it was crazy but it beat the alternative. She dropped her pistol on the floor and got on her knees with her hands behind her head.

"I wish all jobs were this easy," Blakelock muttered.

"Arrest her. I'll get the GHOST FIRE drive," said Blakelock as he motioned to one of the soldiers.

"Why not just shoot her?" asked the soldier.

"No, according to our files she knows Simon Kane which makes her useful to us. Better to take her and the file to Vulcan Base where she can be interrogated," said Blakelock.

The soldier nodded and removed a pair of handcuffs as he walked over to Sasha. Sasha kept her eye locked on the smoke bomb dangling from his belt as he approached. When he was close enough he reached for Sasha's arm. However, Sasha quickly pulled the pin out the grenade and kicked the man with all of her strength causing him to stumble back towards Blakelock and the others.

Before any of them could react the smoke bomb exploded, filling the room with thick gray smoke. Sasha quickly picked up her pistol and ran towards the window shooting at it, causing it to shatter. She holstered the pistol and jumped out the window back first. As she fell she pulled out the grappling gun and fired it upwards, hoping that it would grab onto something sturdy and arrest her fall. Suddenly, there was a sharp tug and she stopped falling. However, she began swinging towards the building.

As she swung closer to the building she pulled out her pistol with her free hand and fired several shots at the window, shattering it. Sasha swung into the building and let go of the grappling hook once inside. Using her acrobatic skills she rolled on the floor upon landing. Finally she took a deep breath, glad to still be alive and surprised that her scheme actually worked. She walked over to the window space and retrieved her grappling gun as it dangled from the upper floor.

Sasha pressed a button on the side of it and the rope detached from the gun, she clipped it to the back of her belt. She looked around and saw a sign that said elevator with an arrow pointing down the hall. She smiled faintly and ran down the hall until she arrived at the elevator and pressed the down button. After a few tense minutes the doors opened and she ran inside quickly pushing the button marked parking garage. As the elevator neared its destination she aimed her pistol at the door, expecting there to be several soldiers in the parking garage awaiting her.

However, when the doors opened there was no one in the parking lot. She shrugged in mild surprise and ran out, expecting at any moment to be shot at, toward the parking garage where her car was. Quickly she got in the car and started the engine, she pulled out of the garage and drove towards the airport. Now that she had escaped, she began replaying what happened in her head. Of the myriad of questions, she was asking herself as she drove to the airport, the biggest question she had was, what did Simon have to do with this?

Watching her drive away from the building was Counselor Blakelock.

"Shall we pursue?" asked one of the soldiers. Blakelock was silent for half a minute.

"No, Project: GHOST FIRE is more important," responded Blakelock. The soldier nodded and walked away, Counselor Blakelock pulled out his phone and dialed a certain phone number. Within seconds he was greeted by the voice of the Networc's leader, a man he and his colleagues knew only as Mr. Zero.

"Sir, you were right. Prometheus Technologies is not the best place to store the file, I'm taking it to Vulcan Base immediately," said Counselor Blakelock.

"Good, keep me updated," said the electronically scrambled voice of Mr. Zero before abruptly hanging up.

Counselor Blakelock returned the phone to his pocket and left.

# Chapter 7
## Bottom of the Barrel

"Deon! Wake up we're here," barked Simon.

Deon groggily opened his eyes. "Great" he grunted, annoyed at being woken up.

He looked out the window and saw Sankan airport in and the city itself coming into view. The plane touched down smoothly on the tarmac. Once the plane had stopped the pilot opened the door and they disembarked. Sankans only airport consisted of a rundown hangar and a dilapidated office building that was built by the Japanese during World War Two and abandoned by them in 1944. A control tower was built by the Vasilev Syndicate in the seventies.

Parked in front of the hangar was a black car with a Chinese man in a suit standing in front of it. Deon followed Simon to the car. As they approached it the man opened the back passenger door for them. The two men got in the car and the driver closed the door. He got in the front seat and started the engine. The back seat of the car was separated from the front by a partition. As they left the airport they drove down a dirt road and entered the city.

"Just when you think you've seen the worst hellholes on Earth," muttered Deon as he looked out the window at the rows of decrepit buildings and haunted, desperate looking people.

Despite traveling the world, during his time with Silhouette, Deon had never been to Sankan before, he had heard about it but nothing compared to being there.

"Tell me about it," replied Simon. "Some of the worst and most desperate people in the world come here to hide or find work."

"So what does that make us worst or desperate?" Deon asked.

"I'd rather not think about it," muttered Simon.

"I hear that," replied Deon. He shifted his gaze to the tallest structures in the city, two skyscrapers across the street from each other.

They both looked the same except one of them had a red pagoda on the roof. "What are those supposed to be?"

"The building with the pagoda on the roof is the Triads base on the island, the one across it is the Syndicates. They divided the city up between them and run almost all the crime in the South Pacific from here" answered Simon.

"Impressive," said Deon dismissively. "So how'd they get you?"

"It's a long story," Simon grunted.

Before Deon could ask for clarification, they pulled up to the front of the Triad building. The driver got out of the car and opened the door for both of them.

"They're in the conference room waiting for you," said the driver before getting back in the car and driving away.

Deon shrugged and followed Simon inside. Upon entering the lobby they were confronted by two large Chinese men in suits. "Pat down," grunted one of the men.

Simon and Deon held out their arms and were checked for any weapons by the men. When they were done, the men nodded at each other and gave them a thumbs-up indicating that they were okay to continue. Afterwards, they walked straight to the elevator and rode it to the sub-basement.

"Didn't know this place went underground," said Deon.

"Yeah, there are at least three floors underground according to Deng," said Simon.

When the doors opened, they walked down a hallway and stopped at a wooden door marked conference room in Chinese. Simon opened the door and Deon followed him inside. The room on the opposite wall was a large computer screen. In the middle of the room was a long rectangular wooden table.

What caught Deon's eye was the seemingly random assortment of individuals seated around the table. Sitting with his feet on the table and leaning back in his chair was tall, strong looking man with spiky blonde hair. He was dressed in a red and green Hawaiian shirt and brown khakis eating potato chips. Seated next to him was an average looking man in a short-sleeved dress shirt with a black tie and gray pants with his head on the table, asleep. Finally across from them was a very tall and attractive woman with pale skin. She was dressed in the black and white habit of a Catholic nun with red hair and a gold cross necklace. She was reading from a pocket Bible.

Upon entering the room the three people looked up at them. The blonde man tapped the man next to him and he woke up slowly rubbing his eyes.

"Welcome back, Mr. Kane," said the woman in a strong Irish accent.

"Thanks, everyone this is the final member of our team, he's an old friend of mine, names Deon Bowman" said Simon. "This is the team. This is Siobhan Costello," he continued while pointing to the red haired woman dressed like a nun.

"The man in the Hawaiian shirt is Mack Roycewicz and the guy next to him is Dennis Faraday," said Simon.

"Simon can I see you for a minute in private," Deon whispered.

Simon nodded, already knowing what Deon was going to say. The two men stepped to the side.

"Simon, are you serious? A nun, a nerd and a guy that looks like a Magnum PI rip off are the team you were telling me about?" said Deon. "You made it sound like this was The Expendables, instead it looks like…like I don't know what it looks like!"

"Hey, what do you mean Magnum PI rip off?" barked Mack sarcastically.

Deon shifted his gaze to Mack and glared intimidatingly. "I ain't seeing a mustache so you must be Hawaii Five O instead,"

"I never liked Hawaii Five O" growled Mack as he stood up and walked over to Deon threateningly.

"Me neither," responded Deon. The two men stood face to face with each other ready for a fight, sizing each other up.

Simon shrugged and jumped between them. "Both of you girl scouts knock it off!"

"Well said," interrupted a smug voice from the door. The door opened and in walked Deng dressed in his usual attire. Deon and Mack looked at each other and shrugged, he returned to his seat, Simon sat at the end of the table while Deon sat next to Siobhan. He looked at her and she smiled back at him innocently, not knowing what else to do Deon smiled back at her. Deng walked to the front of the room and stood in front of the screen casually.

"For those who came in late, you can call me Deng," said the man. "Now that we're all best friends, let's get down to business".

"By all means," said Simon.

"First the basics: You all know that you're here to bring down the Networc," began Deng.

"What exactly is the Networc anyway?" interrupted Mack.

The others flashed him a disapproving look. "Actually, I had a similar question. Ever since we arrived here neither you nor Simon has elaborated on the Networc," said Dennis.

"Yeah, there a reason for that?" asked Mack.

"The reason is that we barely know anything about them," Deng answered.

"The hell do you mean you don't know anything?" barked Mack.

"The truth is that ever since they attacked us years ago, we have been unable to track them down," said Deng.

"So how do you know they even exist at all?" asked Siobhan softly. They looked at Siobhan surprised to hear her speak.

"A good question that can be answered by Mr. Kane. Since he and Mr. Bowman have had direct encounters with them," said Deng. He gestured for Simon to speak as the others looked at him.

Simon shrugged, unsure of how palatable his information would be to them. "The Networc is an organization whose goal, I believe, is to manipulate governments via terrorist attacks," began Simon.

"Seven months ago me, Deon and...a friend foiled a plot by the Networc to steal nuclear weapons from Belarus. Just last month I stopped the Networc from destroying the Aswan Dam in Egypt," he continued. "On both of these occasions, I encountered operatives of the Networc that were in charge of these attacks called Counselors."

"We believe these Counselors, and by extension the rest of the Networc, take their orders from someone named Mr. Zero" he continued.

"That's it?" asked Mack obstinately.

"Not even close, I also witnessed the level of power, ambition and resources that the Networc have at their disposal," said Simon. "Believe me when I say these people have access to an army of highly trained and well equipped soldiers that they are more than willing to use".

"So if these guys are so powerful how are we supposed to fight them if we can't even find them?" asked Dennis.

"The plan is to find Mr. Zero and if we can find him..." said Simon.

"Then we find the Networc," interrupted Deon finishing Simon's sentence.

"And we've been looking all over the world for this Mr. Zero and these Counselors," said Deng.

"And?" Mack asked.

"So far nothing," replied Deng. "However, I have a feeling that we'll find something soon since this is more information than we've ever had on the Networc," he continued. "The important thing now is to wait and prepare".

"That's easier said than done" quipped Mack.

"Be that as it may, tomorrow we're going to be doing another CQB test," said Simon.

The meeting over, Siobhan, Dennis, Mack and Deng left leaving only Simon and Deon in the room.

Simon looked at Deon inquisitively as he held up his head with his left hand and elbow on the desk. "What do you think?"

"Well they're certainly an eclectic bunch but I don't think they're up to the task. Still I'd like to know more about them before I pass judgment," said Deon.

"I'll get you the files on them but I recommend that you give them a chance since they're the best we've got, hell they're all we've got," Simon replied.

"We'll see won't we," said Deon as the two men stood up and left the room.

# Chapter 8
## Life on the Edge

Located in the Cyclades Islands in the Aegean Sea lies the Greek Island of Santorini. It is known for its rugged surface, a result of a volcanic eruption centuries ago. In the center of the island exists a massive caldera. Overlooking the caldera, are Santorini's two principal towns of Fira and Oia. They are known for the white and blue cubiform houses that dot the cliffs of the island overlooking the caldera. The island is a popular vacation spot with pristine volcanic beaches, delicious Greek food and beautiful sunsets.

However, Sasha Molotova was not there for any of the islands amenities, instead she had come here to hide and plan her next move. She owned a cliff-side house in the islands capitol city: Fira. From the outside, the house was typical of the upper class domiciles of Santorini, it was white with a blue dome on top, a pool and a balcony overlooking the caldera. However, inside the house was really a hideout she had maintained for years but hadn't used until now. When she bought it she had the Guild install several secret compartments containing various weapons ranging from grappling guns, assault rifles to pistols, knives and grenades.

The interior of the home was fully furnished with the usual amenities of coastal Mediterranean living. Sasha had arrived on the island the previous night after her disastrous mission in Finland. The first thing she did upon entering her safe house was to get a long hot shower and then go to bed. She awoke in the late afternoon and put on her bathrobe and made some coffee. Several hours later, Sasha sat at her desk in her office and stared at the laptop in front of her. She had spoken to all of her contacts trying to find out who this Counselor Blakelock person was but to her frustration she found nothing.

Another thing she couldn't figure out was how Simon Kane was involved in this. She leaned back in her chair and thought back to the last time she saw him. It was months ago on Sankan, he was telling her about how his wife had been killed by a man named Counselor Black.

"Bojemoi!" muttered Sasha as she snapped her fingers.

Simon told her this Counselor Black person belonged to an organization called the Networc. *Could this Counselor Blakelock be an operative of the Networc like the late Counselor Black?* She wondered.

It was an interesting theory, but she lacked any conclusive proof to verify it and such theories did not aid her with her current predicament. She began to reevaluate her options; she couldn't cancel the job because Silhouette would target her for elimination and her reputation within the Guild would suffer. Besides she was enticed by the challenge of stealing the file. She shrugged, realizing that if she was going to pull this off she would need help.

Sasha briefly considered asking the Smiling Fox for help but chose to use fellow members of the Guild instead because such a heist would be of no interest to her. She leaned forward and pulled out a black external hard drive, given to her when she joined the International Assassins Guild. The drive was fitted with a fingerprint scanner for security purposes. She placed her finger on it and a green light blinked indicating that she was cleared. She plugged it into her laptop and clicked on the drives icon. Instantly, a dialog box opened that said Enter Password.

Sasha typed in the number she was given by the Guild that served as the access code to the Guilds files. She clicked on a folder marked Members. The folder contained files on every single member of the Guild. She scrolled down the list. She figured she would need at least five competent people that she could work with.

As she read through the files she was surprised to learn that the Guild member's codenamed STROBE and DISCUS were killed. She shrugged, since she had no intention of recruiting them anyway. She was pleased to see that the Guild member codenamed MAGIC 44, was still alive though she was dismayed to find that he was already on a mission. She noticed that he was currently working for the Heise She Li Triad on Sankan. She remembered Simon telling her that the Triad was helping him take down the Networc.

Suddenly an idea began to form in her head. She clicked on a folder marked Clients, which contained the contact information for most of the world's major criminal organizations including the Heise She Li. She scrolled down until she found the E-mail address for a man named Mazin Ho. He was the personal assistant for the overseer of the Triads operations on Sankan a shrewd strategist named Deng Shen. Sasha opened her browser and composed a short E-mail, about a paragraph in length and sent it to the personal E-mail address of Mazin Ho.

She clicked send and shrugged feeling pleased with herself. She stood up and looked out the window. The sun was just beginning to go down. She smiled and decided to go for a swim in the pool and watch the sun go down. She picked up her cellphone before walking out onto the balcony. Gingerly, she placed the phone on a small table and removed her bathrobe. She turned around and dived into the pool and swam laps as the sun slowly invisibly continued its descent into the Aegean Sea.

# Chapter 9
## Through the Grapevine

Mazin Ho walked casually to his office having just returned from the break room with a fresh cup of coffee. His office was nowhere near as spacious as Deng's but this was his personal choice. He detested opulence and unnecessary space, a byproduct of growing up poor in the slums of Shanghai. Mazin was a practical man who was willing to do whatever it took for Deng and the Mountain Master. He was a man he had known since his days as an operative for the Ministry of State Securities elite black ops unit Dragon 6. When Dragon 6 was shut down years ago and a kill order placed on the heads of its agents he felt directionless.

That which he had trained to do whatever was necessary to defend had now wanted him, Deng and his brothers in arms killed. Yet they found new purpose when the leader of Dragon 6, who like them was callously cast aside by his homeland, formulated a plan to take over the Heise She Li giving him a new purpose. Occasionally, he wondered what life would have been like if things had been different. He brushed such thoughts aside as he approached the door to his office, eager to get to work. Like Deng and the others he was frustrated by the fact that the Triad had been unable to locate a trace of the Networc.

Even the information Simon had been able to provide had yielded no results. He sat at his desk and brought up his E-mail account, deciding to check his messages. He took a sip of coffee and shrugged not expecting to get anything important. As expected his inbox was empty except for a message. The subject line was blank and it was from someone named KAY. Curious, he clicked on it and was greeted with a message reading:

I KNOW YOU ARE HELPING SIMON KANE LOOK FOR THE NETWORC. IF YOU ARE WILLING TO HELP ME FIRST, I WILL GIVE YOU INFORMATION ON THE NETWORC. SEND HIM AND MAGIC 44 TO

THE THOLOS RESORT IN IMEROVIGLI ON ON SANTORINI ISLAND. I WILL BE IN THE EXECUTIVE SUITE.

- KAY

Mazin sat there stunned as he read the message. There was no way this could be a fake or part of some plot by the Networc. He reached for his phone and called Deng. After a few rings Mazin was greeted with an annoyed "hello?" from Deng.

"Sir, you need to see this immediately, I think we might have a lead on the Networc," said Mazin.

"I'll be right there," said Deng dismissively before hanging up.

Ten minutes later Deng walked into Mazins office annoyed at having been summoned for what he thought was another false lead.

"What is it Mazin?" asked Deng, annoyed. Mazin turned his computer around so Deng could see the E-mail.

As he read it his eyebrows jumped in surprise. He looked at Mazin, "Contact Simon and the others, tell them to meet me in the conference room immediately," said Deng.

"Yes Sir," replied Mazin.

***

Ten minutes later, Simon, Siobhan, Dennis, Deon and Mack gathered around the table in the conference room.

"Anybody know why we're here?" Mack asked.

"Mazin said it was really important," answered Dennis.

"Y'know that doesn't really answer the question," Mack replied.

"Actually it does" said Dennis.

"How?" asked Mack as he looked over at Simon.

"We're here for something really important" answered Dennis sarcastically.

"That's not funny", replied Mack annoyed. Before either of them could speak again Deng walked into the room.

"Bout time," said Mack.

"Exactly," Deng replied.

"What's this about Deng?" asked Simon.

Deng pulled a small remote out of his pocket and aimed it at the screen facing the conference table and the E-mail appeared on it blown up so everyone could read it. Deng waited patiently while they all read the message.

"Who the hell is MAGIC 44?" asked Ben.

"Me" said Mack.

Simon, Siobhan and Deon looked at him quizzically. "What? It's my Guild codename," answered Mack defensively.

"Why MAGIC 44?" Simon asked.

"No idea, the Guild assigns them randomly" answered Mack.

"Anyway, this E-mail is the only lead we have on the Networc so you're all going to Santorini," said Deng.

"I don't like this. Do we even know who this Kay person is?" Deon asked.

"No but I'm sure it's nothing that a professional assassin, two ex-CIA agents and a former IRA super terrorist can't handle," answered Deng smugly.

"What about me?" asked Dennis.

"What about you?" Deng replied sarcastically. "Now just so we're clear, your mission is to go to Santorini and find out what this person wants and go from there"

"I've notified the airport of your flight and they're readying my plane for you as we speak" continued Deng. "So get ready and grab what you need now, you leave in an hour,".

"That's it? No good luck on the mission guys, no go team?" said Mack sarcastically.

"If you want luck talk to Siobhan" said Deng as he walked out of the room.

They looked at Siobhan who looked back at them and smiled warmly. "The Lord will watch over us," she said quietly.

"Works for me," said Simon dismissively as they all stood and walked out of the room.

# Chapter 10
## Watchful Eyes

Unknown to everyone on Sankan Island, Silhouette had embedded three operatives on Sankan. Their orders were to observe the actions of the various criminals and fugitives inhabiting the Island and send that information back to Silhouette's HQ for analysis. To the denizens of the Island they were known as the Flying Fish Trading Company. However, to General Connors their official designation was Task Force 666, though they referred to themselves as the Goon Squad. Two of its members had been released by Silhouette from a top secret section of Guantanamo Bay prison nicknamed Penny Lane.

Their leader was Ben Martin, an African American ex-Force Recon commando turned Silhouette operative had been tasked with leading them. The sniper of the team was Kenji Yamada, a Japanese American ex-Force Recon commando imprisoned at Penny Lane for alleged treason. The team's heavy hitter was another ex-Force Recon commando, her name was Fiona Ramos. A hot headed Cuban American woman sent to Penny Lane for assault, theft and murder among other crimes. Upon learning that Simon Kane had arrived on Sankan, General Connors told them to watch him carefully.

At that moment they were parked outside the airport watching him and four other people board a plane and take off. As the plane took off Martin lowered his binoculars watching it carefully.

"Well?" asked Fiona angry at waiting.

"We're done here, I'm going to notify HQ" said Ben as he started the car.

"It's about time, I hate these surveillance jobs," said Fiona relieved.

"Why because they involve patience?" said Kenji dryly.

"Yeah, I, hey shut up!" barked Fiona.

***

Several Hours later while Simon's plane was refueling in Nepal, Simon and his team were unknowingly photographed by an Equinox agent. The agent sent the photo to headquarters in London where it was relayed to Nigel Solo in Dubai. According to the plane's flight plan it was headed for Santorini Island and one of the passengers matched a description of Siobhan Costello. Nigel grinned at the information, pleased that he would finally be able to leave Dubai and resume the hunt for Siobhan. He had already booked a flight to Santorini and would be there waiting for her, several hours ahead of them.

What Nigel didn't know was that the report he was reading had already been read and copied by an undercover Silhouette agent in the embassy. Having hacked into the embassy computers the agent, codenamed: BROWNSVILLE, had gotten the message and sent it to General Connors at Silhouettes HQ in Langley.

***

General Connors had just returned to his office after having lunch in the cafeteria. He sat down at his desk and saw a message from BROWNSVILLE and a message from Martin. He clicked on the E-mail and read it. According to the message Simon, Siobhan, Dennis and Mack and their new member Deon Bowman were en-route to Santorini. He didn't know why they would suddenly be going there of all places but he wasn't surprised that Simon would recruit Deon since they had worked together as Silhouette agents.

He clicked on the E-mail from BROWNSVILLE in the British Embassy in Dubai. The message concerned an Equinox agent named Nigel Solo that had been tracking a terrorist who had just left for Santorini. Connors read the name of the terrorist he was tracking: Siobhan Costello.

"Oh shit," muttered Connors as he read the name.

According to the Goon Squad, Costello was one of the members of Simon's team. He realized that this agent's orders to kill Siobhan could potentially torpedo Silhouettes investigation into the Networc if he attacked Simon and his team. Connors thought for a minute and considered his options. He shrugged realizing that there was nothing he could do directly, which meant it was time to call in a favor. Connors pulled his phone out and dialed the number of Equinox's Director, Felix Proffer.

After a few rings he was greeted with a surly British "Hello" by Felix.

"Felix, it's Connors I have a favor to ask you," said Connors.

"What is it?" Felix asked.

"You have an agent heading, I'm assuming, to kill Siobhan Costello in Santorini," said Connors.

"I don't know what you're talking about" said Felix.

"Come on Felix, don't jerk me around we've known each other too long," grunted Connors.

"Very well, assuming I do, what about it?" asked Felix.

"I need you to call him off," said Connors bluntly.

"If I may ask, why?" asked Felix.

"I can't tell you, suffice it to say that she's involved in an investigation," replied Connors, annoyed that he couldn't say more.

Felix sighed. "I'm sorry my friend, I can't, this L.A.T. order comes from the P.M. and even if I could I wouldn't,"

"Why? You owe us" asked Connors, stunned.

"This woman is one of my countries deadliest enemies, she has to be destroyed" said Felix. "And for you to ask us to grant her a stay of execution is like us asking you not to kill Bin Laden."

"Felix we've worked together in the past, I'm asking you as a professional courtesy, tell the agent to hold off for a little while at least," said Connors. "Hell we'll help you find her when it's done."

"I'm sorry my friend, I truly am, if this were any other target I would help you. But this woman is far too dangerous to be allowed to live," said Felix.

Connors believed him when he said he was sorry, but was annoyed all the same. "I guess that's it then, see you around Felix".

"And you as well," said Felix as he hung up the phone.

Connors returned the phone to his pocket and considered his options. He had no way of contacting Simon and warning him, not to mention that any support he managed to send would arrive too late.

"Dammit," grunted Connors.

It was a sobering if infuriating feeling that for all of the power he held, there was nothing he could do to stop Simon and his team from walking into the crosshairs of Equinox.

# Chapter 11
## The Nuclear Shuffle

The airport, where the plane was due to arrive, was a small private airport on the edge of Santorini. Nigel was dressed in a black shirt and pants. He had managed to surreptitiously scale the rusted fence surrounding the airfield. Slung over his shoulder, was a Heckler and Koch 433 assault rifle that he had obtained from an Equinox safe house on the island. The gun was outfitted with a scope, stock and silencer. He positioned himself behind a hangar as he waited for the plane to arrive.

Nigel waited patiently for the plane to arrive, after a half hour the plane appeared in the sky and touched down on the tarmac. He flipped off the safety, turned on the guns single shot setting and cocked the rifle. He knelt down and aimed it at the door of the plane. The door opened and out walked a tall well-built man in a Hawaiian shirt, and black tea-shade sunglasses.

"Ahh Santorini," said Mack inhaling deeply as he walked down the stairs followed by Dennis. "Beautiful isn't it?"

"Yes, it's like a postcard," said Dennis as he adjusted his glasses.

Nigel had no idea who these two men were nor did he care. What he did not expect was who walked out of the plane next. Simon and Deon followed Mack and Dennis out of the plane. The two men squinted at the bright sunlight raining down on them. Nigel did not expect Simon Kane and Deon Bowman of all people to be here, let alone to be traveling with Siobhan. The message did not specify who she was traveling with just that she was traveling with several people.

Though he couldn't remember the last time he saw Deon he did remember seeing Simon five months ago in Bangkok. He had said he was going to pursue the killers of his wife, Sheila, so what was he doing working with a terrorist like Siobhan. So distracted was Nigel by these questions that he almost missed her. Siobhan Costello walked out of the plane. She closed her eyes and smiled, her pale skin glistening in the warm sunlight. Standing at the bottom of the stairs was Simon and the others. To Nigel's surprise she was dressed in the black and white habit of a Catholic Nun.

"Well…here we are, so now what?" asked Mack.

"I assume Kay is going to send a car for us?" asked Deon.

Nigel centered the gun on Siobhan's head as she quickly walked down the stairs. His finger tightened on the trigger. He felt the trigger start to move backward when suddenly a small SUV drove up to them blocking his shot. Instantly, Nigel released his grip on the trigger silently cursing the car and the driver.

"I told you a car would show," said Deon looking smugly at Mack.

"Well obviously Kay was going to send a car" said Mack. Out of the car stepped a young teenager.

"Welcome to Santorini, my name is Mikos. I was sent here to pick you up," he said in a thick Greek accent.

"Nice to meet you Mikos," said Siobhan with a warm, friendly smile.

The boy looked over to thank her and his eyes grew large. "Forgive me sister, for my appearance," stammered the teenager as he fell to his knees apologetically.

Siobhan walked over to him and placed her hand on his shoulder and smiled warmly. "It is no problem child, the Lord cares not for how you appear" said Siobhan kindly.

"Thank you Sister," said the teenager as he stood up and opened the doors for them.

"Well that was unexpected," said Mack sarcastically.

"Jealous?" whispered Siobhan in reply as she sat in the front next to Mikos.

"Kind of yeah," muttered Mack while Simon and Dennis laughed at the whole exchange.

Mikos started the car and drove away from the airport.

Nigel cursed himself for not taking the shot when he had the chance. He stood up and flipped on the safety of the rifle.

"Stop!" said an angry voice from behind him.

Nigel turned around slowly. The voice belonged to an obese bearded man holding a flashlight, dressed like a security guard. "Who are you?" asked the man gruffly.

"Oh, I'm terribly sorry Sir, I have my papers right here" said Nigel. He reached for his wallet with his left hand. Cautiously the man approached him, his eyes locked on the gun in Nigel's left hand. Suddenly Nigel hit the man in the face with his right fist, the man fell down on his back unconscious.

"I told you I was sorry," Nigel muttered as he slung the rifle over his back.

He reached into his belt and pulled out a small pistol. Nigel aimed it carefully at the landing gear of the plane. He pulled the trigger and from out of the gun ejected a small device that attached itself to the wheel of the plane. He returned the gun to his belt and pulled out his phone. He pressed several buttons and a map of the airport appeared on the screen. In the middle was a blinking red dot.

He looked up at the plane in front of him, sitting on the tarmac. Nigel smiled, impressed at his cleverness to use the tracking device. He returned the phone to his pocket and snuck out of the airport to his car and drove off in hot pursuit of the others.

***

Mikos drove them to the Tholos resort, he parked in front. They got out of the car and followed him to the Executive Suite. Simon attempted to pay him but he turned down the money and walked over to Siobhan. He whispered several words to her. Siobhan looked at him and then put her hand on his shoulder. They bowed their heads and Siobhan muttered several words. After half a minute they raised their heads, he thanked her and left in the car.

"What was that all about?" asked Dennis.

"His father is sick. He asked if I could pray for him as payment," said Siobhan.

"We need to bring you with us everywhere Siobhan, we'll just pray the pay away," said Mack jokingly.

"You done?" said Simon.

"Not really, no," replied Mack sarcastically.

"Big surprise," Deon grunted.

Simon knocked on the door of the room. In response he heard a muffled yell from outside saying, "It's open" in a familiar Russian accent.

Deon glanced at Simon recognizing the voice as they walked inside. The room was all white with a couch in the middle and a balcony outside with wind blowing through the drapes into the room.

"Nice place," said Mack as he looked around.

As they entered the room a tall, seductive figure in the balcony stood up. They could only see her silhouette as she turned around to walk in. She brushed the curtains aside as she entered the room revealing a face familiar to Simon, Deon, Mack and Dennis.

"I should have known it was you Sasha," said Simon, surprised to see her. He cursed himself for not making the connection between Kay and her codename: KATYUSHA.

"It's been a long time Simon, we really must stop meeting like this," said Sasha with a smug smile.

She was dressed in a dark red shirt, skintight black pants and red boots.

"I thought you were dead," said Deon, displeased to see her.

"Thought or hoped?" Sasha asked.

"Both," grunted Deon.

"Wait, you three know each other" Mack said surprised.

"You could say that," answered Sasha as she looked at Simon.

"This is too rich," Mack laughed.

"How do you know her?" asked Deon.

"We're both members of the Guild," said Mack as he tried to stop laughing.

"What's this all about?" asked Deon sternly.

"Nice to see you too Deon," replied Sasha facetiously.

"Answer the question Sasha" growled Simon impatiently.

Sasha looked at him with a smirk. "Simon you haven't changed, neither have you Deon."

"Clearly you haven't either," growled Deon.

"What's the matter Deon? Still angry about Kingston?" replied Sasha.

"Excuse me, but I don't think we flew halfway around the world so you three could go down memory lane," barked Dennis. They all looked at him, surprised at the interruption.

"The man has a point, why are we here?" asked Simon.

"Very well, several days ago I was hired by a certain...organization to recover a drive from a company called Prometheus Technologies," answered Sasha. "I tried to steal the file myself but I failed."

"So, you want us to help you steal it in exchange for intel on the Networc right?" interrupted Deon.

"Perceptive as ever Deon. It's a shame you weren't that perceptive in Kingston," said Sasha. "The question is are you in or are you out?"

Simon looked at his team, they looked back at him and he could tell what their answer was. He looked back at Sasha.

"I guess we're in Sasha," said Simon.

"Good, as you say let's get down to business," said Sasha.

***

Listening to their conversation from the safety of his car, via a parabolic microphone gun, sat Nigel Solo, *So that's what's going on* he thought.

This new development did upset his plans but not as much as he initially feared. He did know for sure that he couldn't just storm into the room and kill them all since the odds were on their side.

Still with the tracking device he placed on the plane, there was nowhere Siobhan could go that he couldn't follow. Secure in that knowledge, he drove away from the resort and returned to his hotel not far from the airport.

# Chapter 12
## All The Ifs In The World

Dennis never thought that his computer skills would be used to hack into the files of a major tech company, but then again he never thought that his life would have taken the paths that it did in the last few months either. For the last three hours he had been sitting at Sasha's laptop trying to hack into Prometheus Technologies to find out what Vulcan Base was. Mack was busy sleeping on one of the chairs while Simon and Deon were on the balcony and Siobhan was reading from her Bible in one of the chairs in the living room. Sasha sat next to him watching his every movement like a hawk. He would be annoyed if he wasn't so invested in the hacking.

Simon and Deon stood on the balcony looking out at the sea. Simon could tell something was bothering Deon by the surly look on his face. "Deon, what's on your mind?" asked Simon.

He sighed, "I have a bad feeling about this," answered Deon.

"Is it the team?" Simon asked.

"No, it's Molotova," said Deon.

"You never liked her," Simon observed.

"That's one way of putting it Simon, the other way is that she's got a bad effect on you," Deon explained.

"What?" asked Simon.

"Simon I've known you for a long time and I remember how you and Sheila were back when we were in Silhouette," said Deon. "You and Sheila complemented each other, like she was the yin to your yang," he continued. "But Sasha she's different, she gets under your skin like no one ever has. Hell the bitch is an expert at it."

"I don't know how to describe it, it's like she's your mirror image," said Deon.

"My mirror image?" replied Simon quizzically.

"Yeah like an evil twin or some shit like that" said Deon.

On some level Simon knew Deon was right. Whenever Simon worked with her she always ended up betraying them, using them or both. Then almost as quickly as she appeared she would vanish into thin air. However, she always appeared when they needed her and now was no different thought Simon.

"If it makes you feel any better I never trusted her either, but we need her if this is going to work," said Simon.

"Yeah I know that, but I still don't trust the bitch. Especially since she shot me in the ass," said Deon.

"Honestly man, you have to let what happened in Kingston go" replied Simon. "It's been like what, three years since that mission?"

"Easy for you to say, you didn't get shot in the ass," said Deon dryly.

"Hey guys, Dennis got it!" yelled Mack before Simon could respond.

Simon and Deon looked at each other, shrugged and walked in to the room. Standing behind the couch looking over Dennis and Sasha's shoulder at the computer was Mack and Siobhan. Simon and Deon walked over and stood behind them and looked at the screen. The laptop screen showed a diagram of a cube-shaped building with the words Vulcan Base above it. "Anybody want to explain?" asked Simon.

"Well, apparently Prometheus Technologies has this facility on the coast of Northern Iceland called Vulcan Base" began Dennis. He clicked on an icon and a window appeared on the screen. "And this is a blueprint of it" he said gesturing to the computer.

"Cool, and that's where they have that file you want?" asked Mack looking at Sasha.

"Yes, I heard them say it when I escaped," she answered.

Deon flashed Simon a suspicious look, Simon nodded in response.

"So how do we get in?" Mack asked.

"According to this, the facility is too heavily guarded to fight our way in," Simon observed.

"Well, I have an idea," said Dennis.

They all looked at him, curious as to his plan.

"This pipe right here is an underwater exhaust port that is big enough for two people to swim through," said Dennis pointing to the screen. "Down the pipe is a hatch that leads to a maintenance tunnel," he continued. "That tunnel will take you inside one of the Bases engine rooms, from there it's a straight shot to the vault, if you don't get caught."

"That's a big if," said Deon.

"In theory that could work if we could get the equipment," Simon noted.

"Don't worry about the equipment, I can get everything we'll need," said Sasha.

"What are the rest of us supposed to do?" Mack asked.

"The way I see it, two of us go in, get the file then sneak out to the dock and you guys come and pick us up," said Simon.

"So…who goes in?" asked Dennis.

"I was thinking me and Deon," answered Simon.

"Think again, you and me," said Sasha smugly.

Simon looked at her, caught off guard by her statement. "Out of the question, you get killed and we don't get the intel on the Networc,"

"True, but you have no idea what the files name is Simon…and I don't have to tell you," said Sasha.

"She's got you there," said Mack.

"Fine, but I'm in charge," Simon demanded.

The two of them glared at each other, looking for any sign of weakness and finding none. Deon and the others watched wondering who would concede first.

"Then I guess we have a deal," said Sasha as she extended her hand. Reluctantly, Simon shook her hand.

"One question though, where are we going to get the equipment?" asked Dennis.

"I'm going to call one of my contacts right now and set it up" said Sasha. "So, excuse me," she said before leaving the room, closing the door behind her.

"I gotta ask Simon, why are you going?" Dennis asked.

"I used to be a Navy SEAL, so I'm the most qualified for a job like this," answered Simon.

"Which team?" Mack asked.

"Six," replied Simon.

Mack whistled impressed at the answer.

"Any idea who she's talking to in there?" Deon asked.

"How bad could it be?" asked Siobhan. They all looked at her surprised to hear her say anything.

"My God, she speaks," Mack said sarcastically.

Before anyone could respond Sasha walked back into the room. "The good news is that my contact has exactly what we need, but we have to leave now to get it."

"And where is your contact?" asked Deon.

"Riga," answered Sasha.

"Where the hell is that?" Mack asked.

"Latvia," answered Dennis.

"How do you know that?" asked Mack.

"I paid attention in high school," answered Dennis.

Simon and the others chuckled at his answer. "Ooooh, we got a badass over here," said Mack sarcastically as he waved his hands exaggeratedly.

"I'll call the pilot and tell him we'll be leaving," said Simon as he pulled his phone out of his pocket and began dialing.

In less than an hour they were at the airport boarding the plane and getting ready for takeoff. Nigel Solo was at a small outdoor café enjoying some tea when his phone started to beep. Casually, he pulled it out to check, the dot was moving on a course for Riga.

"What could they want in Latvia?" muttered Nigel. He put a small tip on the table, paid for his tea and got into his car. He drove straight to the airport so he could book the first flight to Riga.

# Chapter 13
## Sniper Rifles And Long Stories

After a six-hour flight, they landed at Riga International Airport only to be greeted by the cold air of the night. "Ahhh, so close to home," said Sasha sarcastically as they exited the plane.

"Damn, its cold," muttered Mack as he buttoned his Hawaiian shirt.

They walked out of the airport towards the departure terminal and cars waiting to pick up travelers. Sasha hailed a taxi in Latvian, they got in and she told the driver to head for Warehouse 22 at the harbor. The driver nodded and drove away from the airport towards the harbor. After a short drive they arrived at the warehouse, Sasha paid the driver and he left. The harbor was mostly quiet save for the crooning of ships in the distance. The warehouse in front of them was an old building made of red brick.

"Nice place," Deon said.

"Yeah, for a murder," Simon muttered.

Sasha walked up to the front door and knocked on it. After the door opened, they were greeted by a tall, Caucasian bald man in a green beret, khaki cargo pants and a black sweater. Simon instantly recognized him and he knew now who Sasha's contact was.

"Simon! How the bloody hell are ya mate?" said the man excitedly in a thick, rough sounding English accent.

"Hey Scott," replied Simon.

"You know this guy?" Deon asked in surprise.

"We worked together in Africa, come in!" answered the man as he put his arm on Simons shoulder.

"Is it just me or does that guy look like Jason Statham on steroids?" whispered Mack to Dennis as they followed the man into the warehouse. "Kinda sounds like him too," replied Dennis.

The inside of the warehouse was mostly large rectangular crates that were stacked to the ceiling. At the other side of the warehouse was a small office separated from the rest of the warehouse by a wall and a door. Leaning against one of the stacks of crates was a tall black woman with short black hair wearing a black sweater and blue jeans.

"Oi Naomi, look who's here," yelled Scott as they walked inside.

"She looked up and smiled "Hey Simon, long time no see," said the woman politely in a British accent.

"Hey Naomi," replied Simon casually. Before they could make introductions, the door to the office swung open and out walked a gorgeous young woman with skin as pale as snow. She had long black hair with a white stripe running down the left side of her hair. She was wearing a black dress shirt, red striped tie, white blazer, a white skirt and black high-heels.

"What's up bitches!" yelled the woman excitedly in a thick German accent. She looked over at Simon and smiled a large clownish grin. She ran over to him, lunged at him wrapped her arms around his neck and kissed him on to his surprise.

"Why don't I ever get a welcome like that?" grunted Mack.

"It's been awhile since Tangier, Simon" said the woman coquettishly.

"Yeah well, I've been busy," said Simon.

"I'll bet," Sasha replied.

"I didn't know you knew Gretchen Simon," said Sasha.

"Oh we know each other very well, don't we lover," purred Gretchen as she looked up at Simon with a seductive look in her eyes.

"Gretchen, do you have the equipment I called about," Sasha asked.

"Oh right, yes well before we get down to business allow me to introduce myself," replied Gretchen. "My name is Gretchen Neubauer and these are my two bodyguards slash compadres in crime, Scott and Naomi Grant," she said pointing to Scott and Naomi. "Now who are your new friends Sasha, I know Simon but who are the other three?"

"The man in the Hawaiian shirt is Mack, the man in the tie is his friend Dennis, the black man is Simon's friend, Deon and the nun is Siobhan Costello," said Sasha as she pointed to each of them.

At the mention of Siobhan's name Gretchen stopped and looked at Siobhan then at Sasha. "Wait... wait one heavy metal minute, that is Siobhan Costello?" said Gretchen in excited disbelief pointing to Siobhan. "As in Siobhan the Devil Woman Costello?"

Siobhan grimaced disapprovingly at the name "Devil Woman".

"Yes," answered Sasha, Siobhan smiled at Gretchen politely.

"Why is she dressed like a nun? You know what, never mind this is so fucking awesome!" said Gretchen.

"Mack does she seem a little off to you?" whispered Dennis to Mack.

"Off? Try crazy like a fox," replied Mack.

"First, my favorite badass one-eyed boy toy shows up with my favorite Russian girlfriend and now I have one of the sexiest badasses on the planet!" said Gretchen excitedly. "And she looks like a nun? That's awesome! I mean I don't know why that's awesome but fuck it!"

"Seriously the only way this could get more awesome is if Scarlett Johannsen was with you and said take me Gretchen!" she said excitedly, hands raised to the ceiling.

"I think you have a fan," whispered Deon to Siobhan sarcastically.

"Miss, sorry, Sister Costello I'm sorry I am so fangirling right now, but can I ask you a favor?" asked Gretchen.

"Yes," replied Siobhan.

"Awesome, I heard this story awhile back that you once crushed a brick with one hand. Think you can do it again?" asked Gretchen.

"That's ridiculous no one can do that," grunted Dennis.

Siobhan sighed, "Yes".

"Awesome, Scott we got any bricks around here?" asked Gretchen.

Scott looked at the walls which were made of red bricks and then back at Gretchen. "Maybe?"

"So find one," said Gretchen.

Scott walked behind one of the stacks of crates and returned holding a brick in his left hand. Siobhan held out her left hand and Scott placed the brick in it and stepped back. "Five says she can't do it," said Deon.

"You're on," Mack replied.

"Put me down for five also," said Dennis.

Siobhan wrapped her fingers around the brick and began slowly applying more and more pressure. Even through her shirt they could see muscles on her arm beginning to bulge visibly as small cracks began to appear on the brick. Her body tensed up as her grip on the brick tightened. Suddenly the brick broke in two, Siobhan breathed a sigh of relief and brushed the lingering stony residue off her hands. She placed them behind her back and looked directly at Gretchen.

Deon pulled two five dollar bills out of his pocket and gave them to Mack and Dennis.

"That was fucking badass!" said Gretchen.

"I would appreciate it if you would watch your language Miss Neubauer," said Siobhan quietly.

Gretchen looked at her, a puzzled expression on her face. Suddenly she started laughing. "Too cool, way too cool," she said as she shook her head smiling.

"Thank you all for indulging me, now then onto the business of our meeting" said Gretchen, her demeanor now suddenly serious. "Sasha told me you would need the kind of scuba diving equipment commonly used by the Navy SEALS," she continued while walking over to two rectangular crates piled on top of each other.

"Normally that shit, sorry I meant to say shiznit, is out of my purview," said Gretchen. "Luckily I managed to get some from SOFEX recently," she continued as she placed her hand on the crates.

"In addition to that I was told by the very lovely Sasha here, that you would need heavy weapons and a motor boat," said Sasha as she leaned against the crates.

"Since she didn't specify what kind of heavy weapons you would need I decided to roll the dice and pick something that's fun for the whole family," said Gretchen. She pointed to two cube shaped crates against the wall. "Scott, if you would," said Gretchen.

Scott picked up a crowbar, pried open the crate and pulled out an M249 SAW heavy machine gun in one hand and a Barrett M82A1 sniper rifle in the other.

"Dibs on the Barrett," said Deon.

"As long as I get the SAW," replied Mack.

"I thought the Americans would like those," said Gretchen.

Scott returned the guns to the box and proceeded to nail it shut.

"As for the boat, I obviously don't have that here. However, I can have it delivered to a warehouse anywhere in Europe within a few hours, along with the rest of this hardware and the standard coms, ammo and small arms," said Gretchen. "The only thing left to talk about is price. Now I'm willing to deliver all of this for 50,000 dollars American."

"Fine, I'll send you a check," said Sasha.

Gretchen stared back at her blankly, "Excellent, mein fraulein now where shall I have this all delivered to?" Gretchen asked.

"Hofsos, Iceland" answered Dennis.

Gretchen looked surprised at the answer. "Huh, I wasn't expecting Iceland, it's cool though....literally, anyway when do you need it there?"

"Immediately," answered Sasha.

"Must be something wicked big to have it there so quickly?" answered Gretchen.

"You can do it right?" asked Simon.

Gretchen looked at him, she smiled at him smugly. "Simon, liebling, I'm hurt, getting this stuff there is easier than Lindsey Lohan," replied Gretchen. She looked back at Sasha, "So yeah I can have it there by the time you get there."

"Excellent," said Sasha, the two women shook hands on the deal.

"Well that was easy," muttered Mack.

"Well gang it's been fun but I have to get going" said Gretchen. "Because I'm such a nice person there's a van outside waiting to take you back to the airport"

She turned to leave with Scott and Naomi following behind her. Before she walked out the door she looked straight at Simon and blew him a kiss, waved goodbye playfully then walked out with Scott and Naomi behind her.

"Dude, you hit that didn't you?" said Mack.

Simon looked at him with a sly grin. "Long story,"

"I'll bet," grunted Deon.

"You're one to talk Deon, remember Karen?" asked Simon.

"Who's Karen?" asked Dennis.

"Long story," Deon replied dismissively with a hint of a smile.

"Let's go," said Sasha authoritatively. They followed Sasha outside, true to her word there was a van waiting for them. They got in and drove back to the airport. Perched on the roof of one of the adjacent warehouses dressed in black watching them exit the building was Nigel.

He lowered his binoculars and asked himself what was going on. He just saw a noted arms dealer exit the warehouse a few minutes ago. Obviously there was something else going on but he couldn't figure out how Siobhan and his old friend, Simon Kane, were involved. He shrugged and climbed off the roof, ready to follow Siobhan to where ever she and her compatriots were headed next.

# Chapter 14
## The Judges Of All The Earth

Vulcan Base was established to store sensitive information as well as conduct scientific research. The facility was owned and operated by Prometheus Technologies which was secretly the Networcs scientific research and development branch. Overseeing facilities like Vulcan Base was not a job that members of the Networcs Upper Echelon usually carried out. However, in light of the recent robbery Mr. Zero, the leader of the Networcs ruling council, had personally ordered Counselor Blakelock, a member of the Upper Echelon, to oversee Project: GHOST FIRE.

Counselor Blakelock sat in his office on Vulcan Base's top floor. The office was a large and fully furnished room with ornate wooden doors and a desk. The wall behind the desk had a massive monitor on it used for teleconferencing with the Networcs Board of Directors. The walls were covered with paintings that had been obtained one way or another to furnish the office as well as to make up for the offices lack of a window. Outside of Vulcan Base was the barren, rocky otherworldly landscape of Iceland.

Suddenly there was a loud knock on the door, Counselor Blakelock shrugged knowing full well who it was. He pressed a button on the desk and the wooden doors opened. Into the room walked the facilities chief scientist, Dr. Mysakos Moonbeam. He was a tall man in his late thirties with light gray hair. A native of Greece, Dr. Moonbeam was a brilliant scientist lured into working for Prometheus Technologies in return for funding his research on alternative energy. "What is the problem, now Doctor?" asked the Counselor.

"You've cut funding to my geothermal research lab, why?" asked Moonbeam.

"It is a temporary reallocation of funds, Doctor," said Counselor Blakelock.

"What are the funds being used for?" demanded Dr. Moonbeam.

"That is none of your concern Doctor," said Counselor Blakelock dryly.

Suddenly Counselor Blakelock's phone began to vibrate in his pocket. The Counselor had a good idea of who was calling and he knew that the call had to be answered immediately.

"Doctor, this conversation is over. Now leave" Counselor Blakelock ordered sternly.

"Fine, but this isn't over Blakelock," said Doctor Moonbeam threateningly as he turned to leave for the door.

"Rest assured Doctor, it is," replied Counselor Blakelock as the door closed behind Doctor Moonbeam.

Once Doctor Moonbeam was gone Counselor Blakelock pushed a different button on his desk causing the office doors to lock. He spun his chair around so he was facing the screen. He pulled out his phone, aimed it at the screen behind him and pressed accept. Instantly a blank face appeared on the screen.

"Hello Mr. Zero," said Counselor Blakelock respectfully.

"Counselor Blakelock, what is the status of PROJECT: GHOST FIRE?" asked Mr. Zero, his voice scrambled by the computer so it could not be identified.

None of the members of the Networc from the Board of Directors, to Counselor Blakelock's fellow Counselors of the Upper Echelon, and the Networcs military forces of the Lower Echelon knew what Mr. Zero's real identity was. Whenever they were contacted by him or the other seven members of the Board of Directors all they saw was a blanked out face with an electronically scrambled voice.

"Excellent Sir, we should have the files decrypted in a few more days," said Counselor Blakelock.

"I see, have there been any further attempts to steal it?" asked Mr. Zero.

"No Sir, I've increased security on the vault and I've just had a silent alarm system installed as a precautionary measure," answered Counselor Blakelock.

"Good, make sure that there are no further attempts to steal it, the loss of that file now would irrevocably destroy Project: GHOST FIRE," said Mr. Zero.

"Yes Sir," replied Counselor Blakelock.

"Good, let me know if anything changes," said Mr. Zero.

Suddenly the screen went black and a white box appeared in the middle of the screen that read: Connection Terminated.

Counselor Blakelock turned off the screen and returned his phone to his pocket. He sighed as he leaned back into the chair, relieved that his conversation with Mr. Zero had ended. He felt secure in the knowledge that no one would be able to penetrate Vulcan Base and steal the drive. It baffled him how the most powerful countries on Earth could be careless enough to lose one of the most powerful weapons on Earth. Not to mention that they could be so arrogant as to think they could just cover it up and leave it to rot on the ocean floor.

*Did they even consider the chaos that would happen if the bomb was found by someone else or stolen? But it didn't matter* thought Counselor Blakelock.

# Chapter 15
## All Over The Map

Simon, Siobhan, Dennis, Deon, Mack and Sasha arrived at the warehouse without a problem. To their surprise there was a car waiting to drive them to the warehouse from the airport. The warehouse was a solitary building on the waterfront. The inside of the structure had a small launch that went into the water. Upon entering the warehouse they were glad to see that the equipment had already been delivered and it took up three crates in the middle of the room.

The motor boat was at the bottom of the launch in the water tied to posts on the sides of the launch. Simon and Sasha walked over to the two crates containing the scuba equipment, while Deon and Dennis walked over to the motor boat so they could begin inspecting it. Siobhan and Mack began opening the other crates containing weapons and equipment. Simon began to open the crate containing the scuba equipment but he noticed a small card on top of it. The card read: Enjoy the swim, lover LOL!

Below the message was a kiss in dark red lipstick, the same shade of red lipstick Gretchen wore. Simon grinned as he placed the letter in his pocket.

"You have to tell me how you met her," said Sasha dryly as she handed Simon a crowbar.

"You first," replied Simon dismissively as he took the crowbar and began opening the crate.

"She once hired me to kill some gangsters that stole her merchandise," Sasha answered.

"Naturally," said Simon.

"I gotta say, she might be a weirdo but she certainly delivers," said Mack as he examined one of the assault rifles in the crate.

"You have no idea" quipped Simon wearily as he studied the scuba equipment.

"Mind giving us an idea?" replied Mack.

"A gentleman never tells," said Simon with a smug smile.

"Who says you're a gentleman?" said a voice from the door.

Instinctively they looked over to the door to see who it was. Simon recognized the voice immediately but had no idea what he was doing here. Suddenly the door opened and a small canister rolled towards them. They all instantly recognized what it was.

"Aw fuck," muttered Mack.

There was a loud bang and the world went white. They fell to their knees trying to recover their senses, some of them clutching their eyes and ears. Simon noticed the door open and a man in a gray suit walked into the warehouse. He tried to get a good look at him but his vision was blurry. To Simon's surprise, the man walked past him towards Siobhan. As he approached her, he reached into his jacket and pulled a black object out and aimed it at Siobhan. As his vision stabilized Simon recognized what the object was and what the man was about to do.

As quickly as he could Simon jumped to his feet, grabbed the man from behind and put him in a full nelson. Now that he was on his feet he could see how the others were responding to the flash bang. Slowly they all began to recover their senses.

"What the hell are you doing here?" said Simon as he tried to recover his senses.

Without answering the man stomped on Simon's foot, the sudden pain instinctively caused Simons grip on him to loosen. The man swung around and hit Simon in the face with the butt of the pistol knocking him on the ground. With Simon on the ground, the man shifted his attention back to Siobhan. He scanned the room for her, she was starting to get up and Simon could tell her vision was clearing up. Simon kicked the man on his lower back causing him to once again lose his aim.

He jumped to his feet and grabbed the back of the man's gray blazer and pulled him to the ground as hard as he could. The suddenness of the impact caused him to drop his gun. Simon placed his foot on the man's neck to keep him from getting back up. Now that his eyesight had returned he got a good look at the man's face which confused him even more.

"Nigel, I ask again, what the hell are you doing here?" said Simon.

"Oh God! What was that? I can't hear!" Dennis yelled holding his ears.

"It was a flash bang, don't worry you'll be fine," said Mack who had regained his composure.

"What?" replied Dennis as Siobhan stumbled over towards the gun and picked it up.

"I ask again Nigel, what the fuck are you doing here?" Simon growled, having lost his patience.

Nigel gargled trying to answer. Simon eased off his neck enough so he could speak coherently. "To kill her," rasped Nigel.

"Who? Sasha?" asked Simon confused.

"Me" said Siobhan softly as she walked towards Simon. He noticed that Nigels gun was in her hand.

"What the hell are you doing?" barked Simon as she aimed the pistol at Nigel's head.

"Deng told me this man would be coming for me" said Siobhan as she pulled back the hammer of Nigel's Walther PPK.

Simon knew what she was going to do, grabbed her wrist and jerked it away from Nigel's head.

"Let me go," growled Siobhan.

"Explain first," Simon demanded.

With a sudden jerk of her arm Siobhan freed her arm from Simons grip.

"Don't listen to a bloody thing this terrorist bitch says," barked Nigel.

Siobhan looked back at him regretfully. "That's not me anymore," she said pleadingly.

Simon and the others were surprised having never heard this tone in her voice before.

"If you think that just because you wear that outfit and read the Bible that you've changed Siobhan, then you're insane," said Nigel tauntingly.

"You're wrong" said Siobhan a tear starting to form in her eyes.

"Is that right? So you want to continue this pathetic little charade?" said Nigel. "Fine then."

"All of you," said Nigel as he turned his head to call the attention of the others. He looked back at Siobhan, "Let me tell you about this butcher that you call one of your own," said Nigel.

"Years ago when I was in the SAS this bitch was the IRA's top assassin," began Nigel. "My old unit was sent to take her out," he continued. "She killed four of the men in my unit with a damn paperclip and left me alive so she could torture me for information."

"For two months she put me through every kind of torture imaginable," finished Nigel. "And if you think that's bad wait till you hear about some of the other things she did in the name of freedom,"

"ENOUGH!!!" yelled Siobhan unable to listen anymore.

"Ever since I came out of seclusion everyone has been reminding me of what I did. Asking me if I'm really the Devil Woman, talking about the sins I committed like it's something to be proud of," said Siobhan as tears started to run down her cheek. "Well guess what I'm not, every single day since I left I have had to live with the memory of every single horrible thing I did and I'm not proud of it at all!"

"Everything I have done, since I left the IRA, was done so I could atone for my sins by combatting the evil I once was," pleaded Siobhan as she rested her head in her hands to hide her tears. "And yet, you insist on punishing me for who I once was by reminding me of it and denying that I am still a monster," continued Siobhan as she looked up from her hands and glared downward at Nigel.

"So maybe I should just send you to God and you can ask him whether or not I've changed," she said wearily as she aimed the pistol at Nigel.

"Go ahead and shoot, I'll spend the rest of eternity haunting you just like the rest of your victims," said Nigel stoically.

Dennis, Sasha, Simon, Deon and Mack stood watching Siobhan and Nigel asking themselves whether they should intervene. Siobhan looked down iron sights of the pistol and at Nigel's stern face for almost a minute thinking about what he said.

Siobhan gently lowered the pistol, "No, I only kill the sinful now," said Siobhan her calm composure having returned. She tossed the gun on the floor and walked away.

"This isn't over," yelled Nigel, Siobhan kept walking trying not to listen.

"What do we do with him?" Mack asked.

"If she won't kill him we should. He'll only be an impediment to the job," said Sasha coldly.

"No," said Simon.

"Then what do you suggest," replied Sasha combatively.

Simon shrugged his shoulders and sighed as he looked down at Nigel's face. "Sorry man" he said regretfully, with a sharp sudden blow to Nigel's head, knocking him unconscious.

"He should be out for a few hours. Mack, Deon grab him and tie him up, By the time he wakes up we should be well on our way to Vulcan Base," said Simon.

"Excuse me, are we just going to ignore that whole thing about her knowing him?" asked Dennis.

"For now, yes," said Simon bluntly as he picked up Nigel's gun and placed it in his ankle holster.

Dennis shrugged and walked back to the boat while Mack and Dennis proceeded to tie up Nigel with some rusty chains that had been lying on the floor. Simon turned around to face Sasha.

"Ready to get down to business?" said Simon dryly.

Sasha grinned smugly, "Absolutely, you?"

"Well, it's not like we're gonna say no now?" said Mack.

# Chapter 16
## Death in All Directions

They had been swimming towards the exhaust port for almost thirty minutes. The only thing protecting them from the surrounding cold blue death was the thermal padding of their black body suits and oxygen tanks. Slung over Sashas shoulder was a watertight duffle bag containing their rifles and ammunition. Their pistols were in watertight holsters on their belts. Even though Simon was an expert at SCUBA diving, as a result of his SEAL training, he had gotten used to how eerily quiet it was underwater. The only light was the small flashlights affixed to the sides of their masks.

Suddenly a rocky wall began to appear in front of them. To the left of the wall was the dock with several patrol boats coming and going. Toward the bottom of the wall, near the sea floor, was a small circular opening with a grate over it. Sasha pointed at it with her left hand excitedly to get his attention. Simon nodded in acknowledgement and they swam toward it slowly.

As they approached the pipe Simon motioned for Sasha to back away from the grate. Sasha nodded and swam back from the gate behind Simon. He had been carrying an underwater blowtorch with him, one of the various tools Gretchen had procured for them. Simon prepped the blowtorch and began the arduous task of removing the grate. Carefully he began cutting off the grate, within minutes the grate came off and felt down to the ocean floor.

"Ladies first," said Simon using international sign language.

He could tell she was grinning at his joke under her mask. Sasha swam into the tunnel followed quickly by Simon. The inside of the tunnel was narrow and dark but wide enough that they could easily swim through it. The thick steel walls were covered in rust, it felt like a tomb closing in on them. Just when it seemed like they wouldn't find the access hatch they saw it above them.

It was a round access door with a large wheel on it that they had to turn to open it. Simon and Sasha gripped it and pushed it with their combined strength. They struggled against it for what seemed like an eternity until finally it gave way. They kept turning it until it became easier and eventually swung open.

"You first," said Sasha in international sign language.

Simon shrugged; he swam upward into the maintenance tunnel with Sasha following behind him. At the end of the short tunnel was another hatch. Simon opened it and climbed out of the tunnel into the maintenance room. He turned around and put his hand in the tunnel. Sasha grabbed it and he pulled her out.

Once they were out of the tunnel, they immediately removed their diving equipment and scuba suits. They took a minute to study their surroundings. They were in a large dimly lit room with pipes and electrical equipment on the walls. At the far end of the room was a door that led out of the facility. Simon was dressed in a black turtleneck with a brown shoulder holster, belt and black pants and gloves. Clipped on Simon's right wrist was his wrist blade.

It looked like an average metal armband however, when Simon flicked his wrist backward a small knife would pop out if it. Sasha was dressed in her all black cat suit with a red belt, red gloves and shoulder holster, her long blonde hair tied up in pony tail. Simon pulled out his pistol, a silenced Jericho 941, and cocked it before returning it to his shoulder holster. Sasha did the same with her C96 Mauser pistol.

Sasha placed the duffle bag on the floor and opened it. She removed a silenced KBP 9a-91 submachine gun. Simon was not surprised that she had gotten a Russian weapon for this job, though he would have preferred to use Mp5's instead. Sasha loaded and cocked the weapon then tossed it at Simon. He caught it and slung it over his shoulder. She pulled out another one and did the same. They emptied the duffle bag of everything that they would need, including ammo, grenades and other equipment.

They placed all of their diving and scuba equipment in the bag and sent it down the access tunnel so a guard wouldn't find it and sound the alarm. Feeling ready, Simon and Sasha looked at each other.

"Ready?" Simon asked nonchalantly knowing her answer.

"Always," replied Sasha with a confident smirk.

"Then lets rock and roll," said Simon dismissively as they approached the door.

***

Mack, Dennis, Deon and Siobhan were positioned in the gulf between Vulcan Base and the warehouse on a motorboat. Deon stood at the front of the boat studying Vulcan Base through the binoculars. It was a black, windowless cube-shaped structure on the edge of a cliff, with a dock extending down into the water. The sky was an overcast gunmetal gray with choppy water.

They were waiting patiently for the call from Simon and Sasha to pick them up. Mack was fishing. Dennis was on a laptop waiting for contact from Simon and Sasha. Siobhan was on the far side of the boat looking out at sea contemplatively.

"Fucking hell, its cold," muttered Mack annoyed.

"Well...it is called Iceland" replied Dennis sardonically not looking up from his computer.

"Was that supposed to be funny?" asked Mack.

"That's why it's called a joke," said Deon.

"Not a very good one," Mack grunted.

They laughed at the wisecrack.

"So are we not gonna talk about last night?" said Mack, pointing to Siobhan. Sensing that they were talking about her, Siobhan turned around to face them.

"Is there a reason too?" asked Siobhan.

"Kind of yeah. You withheld important information from all of us. We're supposed to be a team right?" said Mack.

"I hate to admit it, but he does have a point Siobhan, for better or worse we are a team," said Deon.

He put down his binoculars and looked at Siobhan sternly. Siobhan looked at the three faces looking back at her and carefully thought about what to say. "What do you want me to say exactly?" She asked.

"Start with why you didn't tell us about Nigel," said Deon.

Siobhan sighed, "Deng told me that MI6 had dispatched someone to find and kill me and to keep it secret."

"Why wouldn't he want us to know?" asked Dennis.

"I suggest we ask him when we get back to Sankan," said Siobhan plainly.

"You can be damn sure we will," said Mack.

"One other thing Siobhan, Nigel said you tortured him when you were with the I.R.A, that true?" Deon asked.

Siobhan nodded and sighed. "Yes, everything he said about my past is true. But I've changed, I'm no longer a killer of innocents."

They were all silent for a minute, "well as long as we're playing Q and A I got a question for you Deon," said Mack.

Deon looked at him curiously.

"You and Simon have been talking like you know this Nigel guy," said Mack.

"When Simon and I were in the CIA, we used to work with him occasionally, he's a good man but I never knew about this thing with Siobhan" answered Deon.

"So, what do we do now?" asked Mack.

"Wait for the others," said Deon.

"Works for me," said Mack as he returned to his fishing.

## Chapter 17
### Going the Gauntlet

Simon and Sasha walked stealthily through the facility, carefully avoiding any guards or scientists. Despite several close calls, they arrived undetected at the first checkpoint. An elevator would take them to the third floor where they could enter the vault. They drew their rifles, aimed them at the elevator door and slowly approached the elevator. Simon pressed the button on the elevator panel and the doors opened. They quickly stepped inside and Simon pressed the button for the third floor.

As the elevator arrived, Simon and Sasha aimed their guns at the elevator doors, expecting someone to be standing there when they opened. When the doors opened, there were two guards standing with their backs to them walking towards a large vault door at the end of a long hallway. Instinctively, Simon and Sasha aimed their guns at the back of each guards head and fired one bullet each. The suppressors turned the loud crack of a gunshot into a quiet whisper. They walked forward, over the bodies of the two dead men and approached the door.

Next to the vault door was a small computer console on the wall. Sasha motioned to Simon and to the console. Simon nodded and pulled a small screwdriver out of his pocket. Carefully he began unscrewing the panel while Sasha reached into her belt and pulled out a small rectangular device with a black cord wrapped around it. Simon recognized it since Silhouette had its own version.

It was known as a password cloner. Once plugged into a console it would scan it for the correct password and then show it on the cloner's screen. When Simon finished unscrewing the panel, Sasha removed one of the wires and plugged the cloner in to the panel then she pressed a few buttons. The cloner's small screen lit up as the black numbers appeared on the screen changing as the cloner scanned for the correct password. Finally it stopped on the numbers: 997644. Simon punched those numbers into the console and soon the vault door opened.

Simon and Sasha smiled and walked into another long hallway with another vault door at the end of it. Moving about the room from constantly moving projectors were pencil thin red security lasers. They had studied this section on the blueprints. It was easily the most concerning of the vault's security measures. If the lasers path was interrupted, the alarm would instantly be triggered and the vault door behind them would automatically close. The room would be flooded with a nonlethal paralytic nerve gas. At the end of the hallway was a switch that would disengage the lasers; however, the trick was getting through the laser grid first.

"Any ideas?" asked Simon quietly.

"I'll handle it," replied Sasha as she removed her belt and gun and handed them to Simon.

Sasha watched the lasers as they moved slowly figuring out the pattern. Finally, confident that she had figured it out, she got down on the floor on her stomach and crawled forward. A laser crossed over her mere inches from hitting her back. As soon as the laser had passed over her she jumped to her feet and slowly cartwheeled through two lasers.

Simon watched her nervously as she carefully navigated the grid. Her slim frame and years of training as a gymnast not to mention her lack of any loose clothing greatly aided her. Her slow deliberate movements accentuated her sexy curvaceous figure which would be arousing if their lives were not on the line. She saw a laser coming at her, quickly she leaned backward, her hands almost touching the floor. Once the lasers had passed over her, she slowly fell on her back as two more lasers passed over her missing her by inches.

Watching her, Simon was reminded that there was so much he didn't know about her. With her skills she could have been in the Olympics, yet here she was. Sasha slowly slid under the lasers until she was finally out of the grid, she stood up and exhaled confidently. She ran her hand slowly through her long blonde hair and looked back at Simon with a flirtatious smile, knowing that he was watching her. He grinned back at her subtly. Sasha walked over to the panel and turned off the laser grid.

Simon quickly walked over to her and returned her equipment.

"Enjoy the show?" asked Sasha slyly.

"You could say that," quipped Simon dryly as Sasha put her belt and holster back on.

They both turned to face the console, Simon could hear voices on the other side of the door as Sasha began unscrewing the panel. When the door opened Simon ran at the two guards he heard talking. He kicked one of them in the back of the leg causing him to fall backward. Simon then struck him with a sharp blow to his neck knocking him out. The other guard was aiming his weapon at him getting ready to fire.

Simon lunged at him, he grabbed the collar of the man's jacket and hit the guard in his stomach with his knee. As the guard was gasping for breath, Simon tossed him backward against the wall. Before the man could react, Simon flicked his wrist backward causing the knife to pop out of his wrist blade. Simon jammed the knife into the guard's neck killing him instantly. Simon returned the knife to the wrist blade and looked at Sasha.

"Can't let you have all the fun," said Simon sardonically.

"Such a gentleman," said Sasha sarcastically as she advanced forward, ignoring the dead men on the floor.

"I try," said Simon as Sasha plugged the cloner into the console.

After ten minutes the vault opened, Simon and Sasha exhaled, relieved that the hard part was over. The inside of the vault was a large cube shaped room with shelves that went to the ceiling. The shelves contained various boxes and documents. There were even a few paintings that Simon recalled had gone missing from various art museums. Sasha walked around the aisle until she stopped at a box marked Project: GHOST FIRE.

She opened the box and was about to pull out the drive when Simon quickly reached in and grabbed it to Sasha's surprise.

"Give me that!" Sasha sneered.

"What assurance do I have that you'll give me the intel you've got on the Networc if I do" said Simon. "Think of this as an insurance policy."

Sasha grimaced, angry that she had to cooperate for now. Simon placed the drive in his pocket and turned to walk out of the vault with Sasha following behind him.

"Look on the bright side, at least there wasn't a silent alarm" said Simon casually as he walked towards the vault entrance.

Suddenly he stopped in his tracks. "Shit" said Simon as he saw ten security guards aiming rifles at him and Sasha on the other side of the hallway.

"Interesting choice of last words" said a voice, familiar to both of them but especially to Simon.

From behind the security guards walked a tall man dressed in all black. He had the same face and voice of the Networc operative that killed Simon's wife in Belarus, known as Counselor Black, and the operative that he killed in Egypt. Simon had learned from the agent in Egypt that Networc Counselors underwent various surgeries to make themselves look and sound the same. Simon knew he wasn't Counselor Black but seeing that plain face again made his blood boil.

"Blakelock," growled Sasha upon seeing him.

"That's Counselor Blakelock Miss Molotova," said the man.

He turned to face Simon. "Now I must admit Mr. Kane, you are the last person we expected to show up here,"

"I like to travel" quipped Simon.

Counselor Blakelock smirked in amusement. "Yes well, Your travels are over" he said as he raised his hand signaling to the guards to fire.

Suddenly Sasha crouched down on her knee. She pulled out her Mauser and fired a bullet at Counselor Blakelocks hand and another two shots at the guards. Instinctively Counselor Blakelock clutched his bleeding left hand. "Kill the bastards" he yelled.

Simon and Sasha jumped behind the vault doors narrowly avoiding being riddled with bullets in the process. "Any ideas?" asked Simon as he drew his rifle.

Sasha held up two grenades. Instantly Simon understood what she was planning. Sasha removed the pins from the grenades, waited a few seconds then tossed them at the encroaching guards. Instinctively they covered their ears. The resultant explosion shook the room in a loud cacophonous roar and a flash of light. When the smoke cleared Simon and Sasha cautiously peeked out from behind the vault door. Lying on the ground were the guards, some were dead others rolling on the ground whimpering in pain.

"I think you got them," said Simon dryly.

"Come on!" barked Sasha as she ran over to one of the guards and picked up one of their rifles.

Simon followed her and grabbed an M4 from one of the dead guards. The two of them ran out of the vault heading straight for the elevator.

# Chapter 18
## Say When

Luckily the elevator was empty when they got to it. Simon pressed the button for the first floor and to their relief they hadn't shut down the elevators yet. After a ten minute elevator ride, the doors opened and they ran into a lobby. A security guard noticed them running out and began firing at them with an Mp5k submachine gun. Simon turned around as he ran and fired two shots at the guard with his M4. At the end of the lobby was a large door that said docks in various languages.

"I think that's where we want to go," said Simon dryly as they ran toward the door.

Suddenly, two guards casually walked through the door. Sasha ran at one of them before they could react and jumped feet first at him knocking him on his back. She hit him in his face with the butt of the rifle. Then she jumped up and struck the man in the neck with her left hand. Finally, she roundhouse kicked him in the face sending him to the floor unconscious. They opened the door and saw two more guards running at them.

Simon aimed his rifle at them, but when he pulled the trigger nothing happened. Simon tossed the rifle to the floor, pulled out his Jericho and shot one of the guards in the forehead before quickly shooting the other one.

"Simon! Over there!" yelled Sasha pointing to another door at the end of the room.

"Ready to go?" asked Simon sarcastically.

"Only if you are," grunted Sasha.

Simon followed her out the door. Once outside they looked out and saw a dock below them with a ramp leading toward it. They ran down the ramp as fast as they could. Behind them more guards followed, firing at them. Simon pressed the button on his earpiece communicator.

"ROUNDABOUT, this is MONOLITH the party's over its time to pick us up!" yelled Simon.

Over the radio he heard Deon respond "Roger that".

Simon and Sasha took cover behind a crate from the hail of bullets. Simon leaned out and fired several shots at the heads of some of the guards killing some of them with his Jericho. Sasha stood up and fired several short bursts at their pursuers. For every guard they stopped more spilled out of the building like ants from an anthill under attack.

"Fuck I'm out!" barked Simon.

"So am I," Sasha replied as she tossed the rifle to her side.

"Guess we're shit out of luck," said Simon.

Suddenly the heads of one of the guards exploded followed by another. Simon and Sasha peeked out from behind cover and saw an approaching motor boat. Deon stood on the front of the boat holding the Barrett. Behind the wheel of the swiftly approaching boat was Mack.

Simon smiled, "just like we planned".

Once the boat pulled up to the dock, Deon jumped behind cover, while Mack knelt down and drew his SAW and began firing short bursts of fire at the remaining guards.

"What's up bitches!" yelled Mack as he fired at the guards with the SAW.

Deon jumped out from behind cover with an Uzi submachine gun in each hand and began firing as more guards stormed onto the docks.

"Siobhan go!" yelled Deon.

In response, Siobhan jumped onto the dock and threw a knife at one of the guards hitting him right between his eyes. Slung across her back was a model 1886 lever action shotgun. She twirled it around her wrist and fired at several of the guards reloading each time. Dennis had his pistol drawn but mostly kept his head down.

"Sometime today assholes?" yelled Mack to Simon and Sasha.

In response Simon and Sasha ran out from cover and ran as fast as they could to the boat.

Suddenly a bullet slammed into Simon's right shoulder. Instinctively, Simon covered it with his right hand. They looked over at the direction of the shot and saw Counselor Blakelock holding a pistol, fresh smoke wafting out of the barrel. Siobhan turned around and fired a shotgun blast at his face knocking him off the dock into the water. Sasha jumped onto the boat, while Dennis examined Simons wound.

Deon lowered his gun and backed the boat out of the docks and sped away from Vulcan Base. Mack fired at the remaining guards as there speed increased. Finally the base was out of range.

Mack laid down the SAW, "Well that was fun. How's he?" he asked pointing to Simon.

"Fucked," grunted Simon as he clutched his shoulder in pain, his hand covered in blood. He could feel himself slowly beginning to lose consciousness until the world disappeared in a haze of noise.

# Chapter 19
## Rock me Gently

Simon awoke in a bed in a comfortable hotel room. On the far end of the room was a desk and table with a mirror. He was naked and saw his clothes and trench coat hanging on a chair on the far side of the room along with his gun and wrist blade. His first question, was, where was he? He was about to get out of the bed when Sasha walked into the room.

"Good, you're awake," said Sasha with a pleasant smile on her face, which put Simon on guard automatically.

She was wearing a tight dark red t-shirt with a black jacket, black skintight pants and red boots. In her hand was an envelope that she placed on the desk, almost absent mindedly as she walked over to the bed. "Where are we?" Simon asked.

"Kopavogur," answered Sasha as she took off her jacket and hung it from a hook on the wall.

She sat down next to Simon on the bed. Sasha knew what his next question was. "Mack, Dennis and Deon are out at the bars celebrating our success, while Siobhan is...actually I don't' know where she is," she explained.

"We gotta get out of here, they'll be combing the country apart trying to find us," said Simon as he tried to sit up. Suddenly there was a spasm of pain in his shoulder causing him to stop.

"Don't worry about that, we're safe. They probably think we're long gone now anyway and you need to rest," said Sasha. She placed her hand on Simons shoulder softly, the two of them locked eyes on each other.

"Care to show me how they relax in Russia?" asked Simon softly as their faces grew closer.

"Da," said Sasha as their lips touched and they embraced each other in passion.

Gingerly she pulled off her shirt and they embraced each other. She gently lay down on top of him as Simon ran his hands through her long blonde hair down to the hooks on the back of her bra. He kissed her neck softly as he began to unbutton her lingerie. Gently her bra began to fall off revealing her large bosomy chest. As they held each other in sexual desire, Simon didn't notice Sasha's right hand dipping into her back pocket.

"You know Simon this is just like Prague," said Sasha seductively as Simon kissed her neck.

"Mmhm" muttered Simon as she pulled a small syringe out of her pocket.

"Except for a few minor details," said Sasha. She suddenly stuck the syringe in to Simon's neck and pressed the plunger down injecting Simon with a clear liquid.

Instinctively, Simon recoiled from her but he felt his limbs go numb. "You goddamn..." said Simon, his voice already being affected by the drug.

Sasha put her bra back on and got off the bed. Simon stared at her, his arousal replaced with anger. "First the obvious, I've just injected you with a harmless muscle tranquilizer," said Sasha as she placed the syringe on the table next to the bed.

"In a few minutes you'll lose consciousness but in a few hours you will wake up just fine," she continued as she got dressed. "Now for the reason why. Ordinarily a night of passion with you would be very high on my list of priorities."

"However, I have to get this to an old friend of yours immediately," said Sasha as she pulled the GHOST FIRE drive out of her pocket. "Don't worry though, I'm a woman of my word. On the desk is an envelope containing a flash drive that holds all the information I was able to get on the Networc and their connection to Prometheus Technologies," continued Sasha as she returned the drive to her pocket.

"Admittedly, it's not much but it should help you and your friends," said Sasha as she put on her jacket. She walked over to Simon as he lay on the bed, unable to move or speak. "I'm sorry I couldn't stay," she said as she looked down at him.

Simon looked right back up at her, frustrated by his inability to move or speak.

Sasha knelt down and kissed Simon on his lips. When she let go of him there was a satisfied smile on her face.

"I've had a lovely night by the way," said Sasha, as she stood up and walked towards the door.

She turned around to look at Simon one last time before she left.

"Do svidaniya," said Sasha as she blew him a kiss and walked out of the room, closing the door behind her.

*Definitely just like Prague* thought Simon as he could feel himself lapsing into unconsciousness.

***

Two hours later Simon awoke, he sat up in bed, ignoring the pain in his shoulder. He could hear voices from the floor below. Simon got out of bed, he looked at the syringe and tossed it in the trash. He quickly got dressed and walked out of the room, down a short flight of stairs into a small living room with a kitchen adjacent to it. Passed out on a couch was Dennis, watching television on another couch was Deon and Mack while Siobhan was in the kitchen making breakfast.

"Look who's awake," said Mack as he looked up at Simon.

"What time is it?" Simon asked, still shaking off the effects of the drug.

"Ten in the morning," answered Siobhan.

She walked into the living room and handed Simon a cup of coffee. He drank the coffee and was surprised at how good it was.

"Damn good coffee Siobhan," said Simon.

"Thank you," replied Siobhan with a pleased smile.

"By the way what happened to him," asked Simon pointing to Dennis.

"Couldn't handle his beer," said Mack.

"I know the feeling," replied Simon as he took another sip of coffee. "Where's Sasha?"

"She was gone when we got here. Why?" inquired Deon.

"Don't ask," replied Simon as he took another sip of coffee.

# Chapter 20
## The Wrap up

General Mark Lee Connors watched the sunset over the Caribbean Sea. There was no one else at the hotel pool, which suited his purposes since there would be fewer witnesses. Of all the places he had expected to meet KATYUSHA, the city of San Juan in Puerto Rico, was the last one he expected. Still, the tropical weather and warm temperatures were a vast improvement over his dreary desk in Langley. High above in the hotel overlooking the pool were his bodyguards, agents of Silhouettes internal affairs branch, codenamed Blacklist Protocol.

The agents were Anne Shwiechert, codename: LARIAT, and her boyfriend Jeremiah Cokely, codename: KRYPTONITE. They were watching Connors with two silenced MSR Remington sniper rifles. If

Sasha tried anything they had orders to shoot her immediately. On the ground next to Connors was a briefcase meant for Molotova. Connors checked his watch, she was late much to his annoyance.

Just then Connors noticed a tall rather curvaceous blonde woman in a red dress and a white wide brim hat walk onto the patio. Shwiechert and Cokely saw her and followed her with rifles as she walked across the pool deck. She sat down at the table across from Connors.

"You're late," said Connors bluntly.

"I ran into two friends of yours," said Sasha as she looked up at Connors.

"Who would they be?" asked Connors already knowing the answer. Silhouette had been keeping Sasha under close surveillance ever since they made the deal with her.

"They used to work for you, actually one of them is an ex-Navy SEAL the other is former Marine Force Recon" answered Sasha. "The SEAL has one of these," she said pointing at her eye patch.

"How are they?" Connors asked.

"The same," answered Sasha.

"Not surprising, anyway do you have it?" asked Connors.

"Yes, the real question is do you have what I want?" Sasha replied.

Connors shrugged and placed the briefcase on the table. "It's in here, now do you have what I want?"

Sasha reached into her dress pocket and pulled out the drive. She handed it to him slowly aware of the fact that one wrong move would result in her immediate death.

"A word of warning Sasha, if this drive is a fake and you have the real one, God himself will not able to save you from us," said Connors sternly.

"Then it's a good thing I don't believe in God," she replied.

Connors grinned at the joke as she took the briefcase and walked away towards the door.

"Sasha!" barked Connors as she walked away from him, she turned around, a curious look on her face. "Did you look at it?"

Sasha grinned, "It's none of my business".

"This is," said Sasha as she held up the briefcase before turning around and walking away towards the door.

Connors held up his right thumb signaling to Shwiechert and Cokely to not shoot and come down. Connors pulled the drive out of his pocket and looked at it. It was a black little rectangle with a little silver plug on the edge of it. Connors heard two sets of approaching footsteps. He looked over and saw Shwiechert and Cokely approaching.

"Is that it Sir?" Shwiechert asked.

"All of this frustration over something the size of a matchbox car, it's crazy isn't it" asked Connors.

"Yes Sir," Cokely replied.

"Sir if I may ask, why is that drive so important that you would pay that mercenary to steal it?" asked Shwiechert.

"Do you know anything about nuclear weapons Shwiechert?" asked Connors sarcastically.

"No Sir," Shwiechert replied.

Shwiechert and Cokely looked at each other as Connors ominous words sank in.

"Still this whole thing would make a hell of a movie" said Connors.

"Yes Sir," Cokely replied.

"Who plays me?" he asked.

Shwiechert and Cokely looked at each other unsure of how to answer.

"Whoever you say Sir," Shwiechert answered not sure of the answer.

Connors looked up at them. "That's the correct answer," replied Connors smugly as he placed the drive in his pocket.

"All right, let's go," said Connors as he stood up. "Follow up question, who plays you two?"

Again Shwiechert and Cokely looked at each other unsure of how to answer, they looked back at Connors.

"That's also the correct answer," he replied sarcastically. "Though I must say Shwiechert, I could see Emma Stone playing you" said Connors as he walked towards the door.

"Why Emma Stone Sir?" asked Shwiechert as she and Cokely followed Connors.

"You kind of look like her," replied Connors dismissively.

"Cool," Shwiechert said.

"I don't see it," Cokely muttered.

# Chapter 21
## Sharpening The Sword

Nigel walked into Felix's office at Equinox headquarters in London. When Felix looked up to greet him the first thing he noticed was the cast around his arm and the bruises on his face and neck.

"How'd that happen?" asked Felix.

"To make a long story short they tied me up and I had to break my arm to escape" replied Nigel. "It's all in my report Sir."

"What do you mean they?" asked Felix.

"Siobhan's working with Simon Kane and Deon Bowman as well as two other men," Nigel answered.

"That's…unexpected," said Felix mildly surprised. *So that's too more involved in Silhouette's little "investigation"* thought Felix.

"Sir, does this mean Kane and Bowman are also targets?" asked Nigel.

Felix shook his head. "No, the L.A.T. order only applies to Siobhan."

Nigel sighed, relieved that he wouldn't have to kill one of the few people he considered a friend. "Has there been any chatter on her Sir?"

"She was sighted attacking a research facility with five other people, two of which resembled Kane and Bowman. After that she was sighted at various airports on the way back to Sankan" answered Felix. "Interestingly one of them resembled KATYUSHA,"

*That's very interesting indeed* thought Nigel. "So she's based on Sankan then?" he said. "I'll head there immediately and…"

"No," interrupted Felix.

"Sir?" asked Nigel confused.

"Look at yourself man, you look like hell and I'm not sending a man after the bloody Devil Woman that only has one working arm," said Felix sternly.

"But Sir," protested Nigel stubbornly.

"No, consider yourself placed on leave until your arm heels," said Felix.

"What about the Devil Woman?" Nigel asked.

"We'll be watching for her," said Felix.

"You needn't worry though" said Felix sensing Nigel's dismay. "Once you're healed, she's still yours,"

"Yes Sir," said Nigel.

"Anyway you're dismissed" ordered Felix.

Nigel nodded and walked out of the office, angry at himself for letting her do this to him. He walked to the elevator that would take him to the surface. The elevator opened in a building belonging to a front corporation that Equinox used to fund itself known as Steed Transports. Upon exiting the building Nigel got in his car just as it began to rain. He drove to Kensal Green cemetery at the borough of Kensington and Chelsea.

He walked through the cemetery until he found four graves side by side. The tombstones had the names of the four men in his unit chiseled into it. While he was recovering from being tortured at Siobhan's hands he came across the word survivor's guilt. It means the guilt someone feels for being the only survivor of a tragedy. Nigel disagreed with the definition his psychiatrist gave him.

He chose to define survivor's guilt as regretting that he was unable to save people from a tragedy that he lived through. He thought about the definition as he looked at the graves of his four brothers in arms buried below him. If he was being honest with himself this was the first time he had visited their graves since he joined Equinox, mostly because he didn't like the memories it brought back. However, seeing Siobhan after all these years he started to remember the days of torture and the promise he repeated to himself. A promise to make Siobhan pay for killing them. He stood there looking at the graves oblivious to the rain and lost in his thoughts.

Suddenly the rain stopped and the clouds parted, Nigel looked up and then back at the graves. He shrugged his shoulders and walked back to his car resolved to do everything he could to recover as quickly as possible. So that the next time he and Siobhan met would be the last time for her.

# Chapter 22
## String Puller In Chief

Simon walked into Deng's office, an angry look on his face. It had been two days since they had returned to the Triads building on Sankan Island. Simon had managed to convince the team to let him speak to Deng about the incident with Nigel.

"Is there a problem, Simon?" asked Deng as he looked at several documents on his desk feeling Simon's icy stare on him.

"You damn well know there is," said Simon as he approached Deng's desk.

He could tell by Simons tone that this was something serious. He also had a good idea of what had angered him.

"Well sit down and let's talk about this then," replied Deng calmly as he looked up from his desk at Simon.

Simon sat in the chair in front of the desk, arms crossed. "Well?" asked Deng.

"Siobhan," replied Simon.

"Ah, I see the issue with SABRE...and your problem with that is?" asked Deng.

"Cut the bullshit, Deng, you didn't tell me that she, and by extension us, were being tracked by an MI6 agent with a kill order," said Simon.

"Your point?" Deng asked.

"My point is that you didn't think that I, the team's leader, not to mention the rest of them had a right to know," Simon replied.

"I told her not to tell you, because I wanted to see how you operated as a team when confronted with a surprise," said Deng.

Simon sighed, angry and frustrated at the revelation. "So it was a test then?"

"Yes, and I must say you all passed," Deng answered.

"Great, I'll put the test on my damn refrigerator" muttered Simon sarcastically.

"Don't complain, it all worked out in the end besides Solo could not have been a big enough threat for all of you," said Deng.

"He wasn't, but I know Nigel, he's not going to let this go. He is going to come after Siobhan and us again," said Simon.

"Let him, we have more important matters to deal with than some James Bond wannabe," said Deng dismissively. "Speaking of which, have you looked at Sasha's theory about the Counselors?"

"Yes, it lines up with what I've seen. Still it doesn't get us much closer to finding Mr. Zero," Simon explained.

"All in due time," replied Deng confidently.

"I guess we're through here then?" said Simon as he stood up.

"It would appear so," Deng replied.

"One thing though Deng," said Simon as he leaned forward and placed his hands on the desk.

"You might have founded this team, but I'm the one who actually leads it so let's keep that in mind moving forward," said Simon sternly.

"Are you threatening me Simon?" Deng asked smugly.

"No, I'm advising you," Simon replied with a sly grin.

"Either way this conversation is over," said Deng.

"Whatever you say Deng," said Simon as he backed away from the desk and walked out of the office.

Simon walked back to the meeting room so he could tell the team about the meeting. However, he couldn't help but admit Deng was right. If Sasha's theory was true then it was a massive lead in their investigation of the Networc. He was still somewhat irked by being lied to but again Deng was right, the team did work well together. However, a scary thought occurred to Simon, *this was the third time he had foiled one of the Networcs plans so what happens when they decide to retaliate?*

Thank you for reading Never Say Forever.
Please post a review on Amazon.com for the
author.


Check out other books in the
Shadow World Series
Sanction Blue
Edge of the Abyss
Hell to Pay
Death Dealers Incorporated
No One Lives Forever


The Networc strikes back with a vengeance in
Book Seven of the Shadow World Series:
Vengeance Is Forever...

CPSIA information can be obtained
at www.ICGtesting.com
Printed in the USA
BVHW031521041122
651158BV00012B/1418